23

-THE FALL OF THE-

HOUSE OF TATTERLY

-THE FALL OF THE-

HOUSE OF
TATTERLY

SHANNA MILES

**union
square
kids**

NEW YORK

**union
square
kids**

NEW YORK

UNION SQUARE KIDS and the distinctive Union Square Kids logo are trademarks
of Union Square & Co., LLC.

Union Square & Co., LLC, is a subsidiary of Sterling Publishing Co., Inc.

Text © 2023 Shanna Miles
Cover art © 2023 Union Square & Co., LLC

ISBN 978-1-4549-4930-5 (hardcover)
ISBN 978-1-4549-4932-9 (paperback)
ISBN 978-1-4549-4931-2 (e-book)

Library of Congress Cataloging-in-Publication Data

Names: Miles, Shanna, author.
Title: The fall of the House of Tatterly / Shanna Miles.
Description: New York : Union Square Kids, 2023. | Audience: Ages 8–12. |
    Summary: "In a magical modern-day Charleston, twelve-year-old medium
    Theo must dodge witchy aunties, an occasionally possessed cousin, and
    some ghostly grandparents to save his family from a demon with a
    grudge"—Provided by publisher.
Identifiers: LCCN 2022047501 (print) | LCCN 2022047502 (ebook) | ISBN
    9781454949305 (hardcover) | ISBN 9781454949329 (paperback) | ISBN
    9781454949312 (epub)
Subjects: CYAC: Mediums—Fiction. | Supernatural—Fiction. | LCGFT:
    Paranormal fiction. | Novels.
Classification: LCC PZ7.1.M55668 Fa 2023 (print) | LCC PZ7.1.M55668
    (ebook) | DDC [Fic]—dc23
LC record available at https://lccn.loc.gov/2022047501
LC ebook record available at https://lccn.loc.gov/2022047502

For information about custom editions, special sales, and premium purchases,
please contact specialsales@unionsquareandco.com.

Printed in the United States of America

Lot #:
2 4 6 8 10 9 7 5 3 1

08/23

unionsquareandco.com

Cover art by Ronique Ellis
Cover design by Marcie Lawrence
Interior design by Rich Hazelton

For Tate and Bryce,
the most magical boys on the planet

I remember pap tellin' me 'bout stretchin' vines acrost roads and paths to knock de patterollers off deir horses when dey were tryin' to ketch slaves. Pap and mammy tole me marster and missus did not 'low any of de slaves to have a book in deir house. Dat if dey caught a slave wid a book in deir house dey whupped 'em.

—Lizzie Baker, Adams-Hunter,
North Carolina, 1936

SLAVE NARRATIVES:
A Folk History of Slavery in the
United States from Interviews with Former Slaves
(Washington, DC: Federal Writers' Project, 1941)

Chapter 1
Billy's Bad End

Theo was alone again. His aunts would be upset if they saw him sitting by himself. They thought he spent too much time alone, that he was too quiet for his own good. They worried, but Theo wasn't thinking about that at the moment. It was true, though: he *was* too old to be swinging by himself on the playground. But the other guys weren't like him; they were normal. They couldn't see what he saw, which was the boy swinging beside him. The dead boy. Theo had a gift for communicating with the dead. He could sense spirits even better than his aunts, especially ghosts who'd been around awhile.

He should have known this was going to happen. When he woke up that morning there were ten garden snails stuck to his bedroom window and a hand-sized moth trapped in the light of his ceiling fan. Great-Aunt Trudy Anne, who

1

had been dead quite a long time, told him that it was a bad omen, and Aunt Ionie, who was very much alive, said she'd meditate for a vision about said garden snails. Both of them told him to come straight home after school.

He didn't listen.

Instead he packed some light exorcism supplies, just in case he had to do a quick exorcism on the fly. A little warding salt: part cherrywood ash, black salt and black pepper; some Florida water, which wasn't from Florida at all; and his Daniel shot—the basics. It wasn't that he felt compelled to help *every* ghost he came across, but some ghosts, especially kid ghosts, were a sore spot. If he didn't help, who would? He packed everything in a white JanSport he called his magipack. *Magic + pack*, get it? Well, *he* thought it was clever.

"What's your name?" Theo asked the boy ghost. He was swinging his nearly translucent legs up in the air. To any normal person passing by the park, it just looked like the wind was blowing, except it wasn't. For a second a chill ran through Theo's bones.

"Billy," the boy replied.

Theo told Billy his name and pushed in his earbuds. There wasn't anything playing, but if anyone saw him they'd just assume he was reciting lyrics and not talking to the air. He pulled out a soda bottle from his backpack and pretended to drink, then unscrewed the cap and poured the Florida water into a little puddle on the ground to help with the transition from this world to the next. It was his aunt Cedella's recipe, and he'd let it cure in a copper pot under three full moons like she'd told him. He hoped it would work. This ghost had been around for decades. He could tell by the orange turtleneck and bell-bottoms that Billy had been playing in the same spot since before some of his aunts were born.

"You must be new," Billy said. "Sometimes Philip comes by the park to play. He dresses funny like you."

Theo nodded, remembering the faded pictures of Philip Gray posted on the lampposts near the basketball court. He'd gone missing the year before. Theo would like to help him too, but he couldn't get a handle on where he liked to haunt. Some ghosts were wanderers like that, hopping from the place they died to a handful of other sentimental places; others liked to stay in one spot forever. In either case, the haunting spot is a place they know, and it has to have a strong connection to their lives.

"I think I might just be new to you. Why do you like this park so much? It doesn't seem so special to me."

"Well, that's where you're wrong, buddy," Billy said as he jumped off the swing right into the puddle of Florida water and proceeded to give Theo a tour.

You had to get ghosts talking if you were going to find a way to get them to remember. As Billy talked, Theo could see the outline of what the park used to look like. The rubber mat changed back into a pit of tree bark and then a sandbox and then a slab of concrete. The plastic corkscrew slide grew and stretched into a ten-foot-tall metal death slope, and right beside it bloomed a gleaming geometric dome. Between the jungle gym bars of Billy's crystallized memory, Theo could just make out the guys playing basketball in the present.

"Perfect for hanging upside down!" Billy exclaimed as he climbed. Clarity hit Theo in the chest as he realized this was how it happened.

"Do you remember the last time you were here?" Theo asked, his eyes beginning to move between Billy and the other guys on the basketball court on the opposite side of the park. Good. They weren't paying him any attention. They probably hadn't even noticed he hadn't come back from the bathroom.

Billy hovered a bit, high in the air, his knees resting on two thin rusting metal bars. As Theo watched, the skids and squeaks of the sneakers on the court got quieter. The dome began to glow and become more solid. Billy, no longer alone, was surrounded by other kids, swinging, hanging from their arms, or upside down on a single leg. Billy flipped upside down too.

"Yeah, I do. I was playing with my friend Carl. He dared me to see if I could jump from one bar to the other like Tarzan," Billy said.

Theo swallowed. He hoped he wouldn't have to see Billy die. Sometimes that happened, just before they made their way to the other side. He knew it was just a replay of what went down and not the real thing, but that didn't always make it any better. His instincts were to yell and tell him to stop, climb the dome himself and grab Billy's hand, but he couldn't. This had already happened. This was the past. Theo pulled out a piece of Bubble Yum from his pocket, the last in the sleeve, and chewed furiously.

"You're up kinda high," Theo said. He put his hand over his eyes to shield them from the late-afternoon Charleston sun. The temperature dropped at least ten degrees as Billy laughed and leaped, his arm stretching for a bar. His fingers just barely grazed it.

Theo's heart skipped when Billy missed, and a nervous, churning feeling gripped his gut as Billy plummeted headfirst toward the concrete. But this time his body didn't break as it hit the ground.

It disappeared.

Theo heard something like a cross between a scream and a bark, and for the briefest second it felt like something furry was walking through his legs, its tail brushing against his skin. Theo looked down and then turned and frowned. There was nothing there, at least nothing he could see—and he could see more than most, more than he wanted to. Must have been one of those playground spirits, Huggin' Hannah or Flying Farrah.

Theo whipped around as someone grabbed him from behind. He twisted but couldn't shake them off. Then that bark was in his ears, loud and vicious, ready to attack.

"Get off me!" Theo yelled.

"Aye, who are you talking to?"

Theo turned, breathing hard, his arms suddenly free. "What?"

"I said, who are you talking to? You yelled." Theo's friend Frank bounced his basketball on the sidewalk. Theo blinked. The playground was just like it was before, empty, save for one rocking swing.

"You okay?" Frank asked as his freckly forehead wrinkled. Some of the kids called him Spots, because of the absolute riot of freckles on his face, but it felt kinda mean to Theo, so he just called him by his name, or Baskets, or bruh, or Freehand or Fam Fizzle or anything besides Spots.

"Uh, yeah."

"You don't look okay. You look shook."

Theo leaned back and laughed weakly. "Never that! I'm breezy. I'm cool. I'm good. Really."

"Aight, I was just letting you know that Coach Lattimer is starting tryouts a week from Monday, if you're still interested in joining the team."

"I am."

"Nah, you're too busy listening to Ariana Grande mixes," Frank teased as he tried and failed to snatch one of

7

Theo's earbuds. Theo dodged, and the two boys shadow-boxed for a minute.

"You just mad I won't let you get on one of my custom beats," Theo joked. He'd replay the conversation back in his mind later to make sure he sounded self-assured and easy when really he was a ball of nerves.

"Whatever. My flow rocks a cappella. Scrubs like you gotta ride the beat like kids on training wheels," Frank said and then launched into one of his raps about Jordans and jelly sandwiches.

Theo picked up the basketball and threw it. Frank caught it in the chest and tumbled back a bit.

"Practice. But you gotta be focused for tryouts. You can't, um . . . you know." Frank paused for effect, and Theo knew it was about his habit of "spacing out," as the guys called it. "Uh, just be ready next Monday at four."

"Aight. I gotta see if my cousin can pick me up after."

"Not a problem. Just wear gym clothes and be ready to play."

"I'll be ready," Theo replied.

"You think your cousin Issa will be there?" Frank asked.

"Why would she come to basketball tryouts?"

"I don't know. To w-watch, m-maybe," Frank stuttered and cleared his throat.

"You like her!" Theo shouted.

"I didn't say all that."

"Bruh, you didn't have to. You like Issa! For real?"

"I didn't say that!" Frank yelled back, his tawny cheeks turning as red as his bushy hair.

"I mean, I'm not judging. You can call her. How 'bout I text her right now?"

"No!" Frank yelled. He went to grab Theo's phone, but Theo pulled it out of reach just in time. Theo smiled and put his phone back into his pocket.

"I . . . uh . . . I mean, nah, uh. I'm good," Frank said, obviously trying not to seem overeager.

Theo knew his cousin was cute, but he didn't feel the need to be overprotective of her. She got herself into too much trouble for him to take on that role, but Frank seemed okay. If she liked him, she liked him, and if she didn't, she wouldn't have any trouble letting him know.

Frank changed the topic to Tekken characters and which gaming chairs were the best, and it wasn't too long before he was saying good-bye, his knuckle to Theo's, and left. Theo waited until he was out of sight to see if he could still feel Billy's presence, but he couldn't. He'd missed his chance. He'd screwed up, and he wasn't sure if he was going to be able to fix it. He'd just have to sneak out of his room later. He sniffed the air for the smell of sour milk and rotten eggs, a sure sign of bitter magic, but could only catch the hint of Charleston's paper mill on the wind and coffee from the nearby bookshop. Yeah, he'd come back later, even if he really didn't want to.

Chapter 2
A Bright Morning

Theo's entire family had supernatural powers, and many of them lived together in the old family mansion on East Bay Street in Charleston: Theo; his great-grandmother, whom everyone called New Nana; his aunts; his cousin Femi; and occasionally his second cousin Issa, when her parents were traveling, all occupied rooms in the family house. They were all his father's family. His aunt Roneisha had formally adopted him, but everyone had a hand. Theo's dad had died before he was born, and his birth mom, Cree, had given Theo up to the aunts a few weeks after he was born. Since then, his birth mom sometimes would show up out of nowhere, stay for a few days, then leave as quickly as she'd arrived. He didn't like to think about her. Besides, there was a lot of girl energy in the house. Sometimes too much. Femi's dad, his uncle Yomi, was in the custody of the Global Magic Authority, or the GMA, for something that had to do with the Eternal Wars. There was also another uncle, his granddad's brother, somewhere in South America, but for the most part home was auntie central.

It was a big house, a really big house that real estate agents were always hounding them to sell, but everyone was as tied to the place as the devil's ivy creeping up and into the brick on all sides. It had three floors with high ceilings and antique chandeliers with medicinal and magical herbs hanging from them. There was a garden, a defunct fountain that attracted all kinds of magical birds if you made the mistake of filling it with water, and the well-worn steps of a home used to feet of the same blood. There was even a carriage house out back where his aunt Sabrina lived so she could play Fela Kuti all night long and invite her artist friends to make pots or spellcast into her paints at five in the morning.

His great-great-grandfather Samuel Tatterly was the first to paint the house its particular shade of haint blue. Most Carolinians just painted their porch ceilings that color to ward off evil spirits, but if a ceiling is good, a whole house has got to be better. The Tatterlys had passed the place down from generation to generation since the

nineteenth century, and had lived on the property for gen-
erations more before then as enslaved people. The house
was as much a part of them as their own names.

Theo woke up trying to think up the punchline to
a joke, something about ghosts and garden tools, but it
wasn't coming to him even though there were more snails
on his window this morning. He was rushing because he
was late again. If he wanted to bum a ride to the gym
with Aunt Cedella, he had to get up with the sun. She
always left early. He'd overslept because he never woke
up with an alarm. It disturbed Great-Aunt Trudy Anne
during her Bible study time. She liked early mornings
best for her reading. Of course, he could have ignored
her—she was a ghost, after all—and used an alarm clock
like everyone else, but Theo was kind to the spirits he
had to live with.

"You went out last night," Great-Aunt Trudy Anne
chastised. She was sitting in an old rocking chair, her
reading glasses perched on the tip of her nose. The rose-
gold morning light was filtering onto her wispy image
from the window. Theo was about to reply when he
heard voices outside. He sidestepped his aunt's ghostly
form and opened the window carefully so the snails

dropped off gently instead of being smushed. There was someone sniffing around in Aunt Cedella's herb garden.

"This is private property!" he shouted down.

"Oh, uh, good morning!" the woman said. She wore a khaki skirt and button-down shirt, and a man in a powder-blue seersucker suit was with her. They looked like a couple, but they were probably real estate agents.

"I'm gonna guess you already rang the bell and my auntie told you we're not selling."

"Yes, but this is the perfect house. I mean, we could offer you . . ."

"There's poison ivy in the garden," Theo lied, and the couple jumped back. Of course there were poisonous plants out there—nothing they'd have to worry about just walking by, but he wasn't going to tell them that. Theo slammed the window closed and turned to Great-Aunt Trudy Anne.

"You gonna tell?" he asked as he yawned, wiping the eye boogers off his face.

"Do I ever?" she asked. "Ionie had a vision, so I 'spect you won't be gettin' out too much now that a hag done got to you."

Theo pressed his fists to his eyes and sighed dramatically. It was embarrassing. He'd let a simple playground demon shake him. Huggin' Hannah was known to catch all the underage Bikin, or magic folk, at one time or another. If she did, though, you were supposed to shake it off and pretend nothing happened. You definitely didn't tell anyone about it. But was that really it? And since when did Huggin' Hannah use hellhounds? This Billy situation was turning out to be more than he bargained for. Not to mention how sensitive the aunts were to visions since the untimely death of their brother, Theo's dad.

"How do you know everything? You don't even leave the house," Theo said as he yawned again and then shuddered at the smell of his own breath.

"Don't worry about all that. Just know that I know."

"Auntie didn't say anything to me about a vision," he said.

"Oh, no, she won't be sharing this one. This one's a secret," Trudy said as she slowly faded out of sight.

"Then why'd you say anything? Now I'll be thinking about it all day," he shouted.

Great-Aunt Trudy Anne had been dead for nearly half a century, as had her brother, Nathaniel Tatterly, who liked to bark Bible verses at him while he brushed his teeth, and Old Nana Tatterly, who helped him with his math homework. They weren't the only ghosts that lived in the Tatterly home, but they were his favorites and the ones he saw most often. Not every ghost needed help passing on, like Billy; some stuck around for personal reasons. The easiest way to tell the difference was whether or not they knew they were dead.

"Just thought you'd like to know," Great-Aunt Trudy Anne said, her head fading back into view and floating disembodied right above his underwear drawer. "'Sides, you need to be more careful. I've been hearing whisperings about restless spirits, roaming children. I don't want you caught on the wrong side of a demon."

"I can take care of myself—for the most part."

Great-Aunt Trudy Anne laughed. "Boy, I done forgot more than you think you know. Caster Cucuy, Nightwalkers, the Pat Roller, the Moon Ax Child, Oak Singer, the Drowned Girl, Yellow-Eyed Warblers, Inkanyamba, Grootslang . . ."

"Okay. I get it," Theo whined.

"You think you do. Better wise up, boy, 'fore you find yourself on the bad end of a bad cast out. Don't put yourself or this family in danger 'cause you think you the only medium still workin' in this house. Ro will be back by the end of the month and she doesn't need to find her son on the bad end of a crooked street."

"Yes ma'am."

"Theo! You better be dressed!" Aunt Ionie yelled from the first floor. Theo loved his aunts more than anything. He didn't really know why Cree had given him up but Ro and her sisters had stepped in. Roneisha, who everybody called Ro, was who he really considered his mother, even if tracking down magical artifacts took her away for weeks at a time. While she was gone, the aunts showered him with more love than one kid could ever ask for.

"Coming!" Theo yelled as he did a final check of himself in the mirror. White Nike Dunks with the extra-fat white laces? Check. White jeans with deep pockets for talismans, Bubble Yum, and brick dust? Check. Powder-white button-down oxford shirt with all buttons buttoned? Check. Granddaddy's old wooden cross necklace? Check.

He nodded at himself in the mirror. He looked pretty good. White was the easiest way to ward off bad spirits. It was his first line of defense. In his duffel he had a few white T-shirts and dove-colored basketball shorts. The second line of defense was the small plastic baggie of brick dust and warding salt he kept in his right pocket at all times. A tiny line against the doorway of any room he was in would keep away harmful spirits. His granddaddy's necklace might seem like overkill to some—his aunt Cedella thought so—but Theo liked to call it being prepared. He was a medium. He could talk to ghosts, and if the conditions were right, he could send them on to their next stop on the soul train, wherever that was.

"You look nice today," Aunt Cedella mentioned as he made his way to the breakfast table. She had huge honey-hazel eyes and always wore her hair in an extra tight bun that made her eyebrows lift so she looked surprised even when she wasn't.

"Thank you. So do you. I like that dress, and your hair looks really shiny today," Theo replied. Aunt Cedella eyed him suspiciously from her seat at the breakfast table, and he noticed how much she looked like the picture of his great-great-great-aunt. The picture was sitting on one of the shelves on their ancestor wall. They both had the same half smile. Aunt Ionie was sitting opposite her with a soup bowl–sized cup of coffee.

"Thank you, and no, you cannot ride with me to the gym today, if that is what you're buttering me up for."

Theo threw his hands up in frustration. "Why?!"

"I have to go in early to meet one of my students for a conference. Femi can take you," she said.

Theo scowled and made a big show of slamming the cabinet doors a little too hard as he made himself a bowl of cereal: Rice Krispies with bananas and chocolate chips, steering clear of New Nana's dried herbs, flowers, and jars of graveyard dirt. If he wasn't careful, he could easily mistake a jar of cat bones for marshmallows.

"Don't be disrespectful to the house just because you can't get up on time," Aunt Ionie murmured between sips of her coffee. She, like him, favored an all-white look every day of the year, regardless of the occasion. She also had a mole right between her eyes that Great-Aunt Trudy Anne claimed marked her for second sight. A sea of papers was strewn out before her, along with the Book of Ages, the family Bible, and a spirit journal.

Theo stuffed a handful of dry cereal into his mouth from the box and chewed loudly. "You know, Great-Aunt Trudy Anne hates the alarm," he said through mouthfuls.

"Trudy Anne is dead. She doesn't get to make demands anymore," Aunt Ionie said flatly as she riffled through old folders and envelopes. Some of them were so old they were yellowed and thin as onionskin. "There has got to be a formal deed in here," she whispered.

Every living person in the house knew about Trudy Anne and the other ghosts. While Theo was currently the only working medium in the family, he was not the first. New Nana, in her day, was supposed to be one of the best, but she'd stopped working since her last stroke. She couldn't talk anymore and spent a lot of time with Femi, who didn't need her to speak to communicate because he could read minds.

"I saw some real estate agents in the garden this morning," Aunt Ionie murmured as she picked up a highlighter and marked something on one of the papers.

Aunt Cedella rolled her eyes. "They gettin' bolder and bolder. Ionie, all you gonna do is stress yourself out. I put a charm on all the documents down at city hall, so I know when they've been accessed. We've been here before."

"This time feels different. It's not just nosy real estate people. It feels like bitter magic."

Aunt Cedella laughed. "I've never heard of a property demon. Or maybe you think it's some civil law evil eye at work. They just can't take that we own this place. Plain and simple."

"Whatever it is, I'd feel a lot more comfortable if I could find the original deed with the Tatterly name in black and white." Aunt Ionie frowned as she searched, and Aunt Cedella matched her. For a second they looked like identical twins instead of fraternal.

Aunt Cedella could see auras and manipulate emotions. She owned a bakery just a few miles from the house, where she cooked good feelings into cakes, cookies, and other pastries. The old families in Charleston who knew about the Tatterlys sometimes made private orders. You wouldn't want to get a slice of Cedella's truth pecan pie if you'd ever done anything wrong in life. She had a sign made for the house with the family name cast in bronze, and the bakery had old pictures of the family and the house going back to the nineteenth century on the walls. There was pride in the Tatterly name.

Aunt Ionie slurped her coffee again and gave Aunt Cedella a look, like they shouldn't be talking about the house. She had a massive gift for premonition, which meant she could see the future. And she had a mild ability in telekinesis, which meant she could move things with her mind. She couldn't lift a car or anything, but she could definitely send a spoon flying across the room to smack your knuckles when she had a mind to. Which she did. Theo had a habit of putting too many chocolate chips into his cereal, and Aunt Ionie wouldn't have it.

"That hurt!" Theo whimpered.

"Watch the chocolate," she said without looking up from the mess of papers. His phone buzzed in his pocket, and he quickly shot off a reply to his cousin Issa.

> Billy make it ova?

> > Nope.

> You losing your edge

> > Never that! I'm sharp as Wolverine claws.

> Have Femi come get me. Ask him. Ask him. Ask him. Mama wants me to go help her volunteer at some community center.

> > Can't. Dungeon Day.

> Booooooooooooooooooooooo

> Text Ms. Katherine. She told Aunt Brina she needed a break from the twins.

> 🙏 Genius kid. Don't believe what they say about you.

> Shaddup

Aunt Sabrina wasn't at the breakfast table that morning—or any other morning. She was the artist and liked to sleep in. She was the youngest of Theo's father's four sisters and had the largest power for premonition and visions, but it wasn't as reliable as people would think.

"Ready, Snot Boy?" Femi teased as he bounced into the kitchen. Femi was Aunt Ionie's son and a powerful psychic. Theo frowned as he finished his cereal.

"Don't call me Snot Boy."

"Whatever, Snot Boy. I don't care how much allergy medication you take. You'll always be Snot Boy to me," Femi teased some more.

"Ssssh!" Aunt Ionie told them both and then turned up the radio she had playing. "Don't you hear Mahalia Jackson singing?"

"You play her every morning. I didn't know we needed to listen in silence." Femi grumbled.

"Maybe you should, so her voice could exorcise your foul mood!" she said and squeezed his cheeks. He wriggled away, pretending to hate her attentions. "It helps me come out of my meditative state on a good note."

"And what did you realize, Mother?" Femi asked in that annoying tone Theo hated. It was like he already knew everything, which he did, but there was a house rule that he couldn't rub it in everyone's faces.

"Nothing that makes sense." Aunt Ionie looked at Theo, and he knew instantly it had something to do with him.

A police siren tore down the street, followed by two more police cars and a van, flashing their red and blue lights and casting colorful shadows across the kitchen cabinets.

"Too early in the morning for all that," Aunt Cedella said.

Aunt Ionie shrugged. "Doin' their jobs, I guess."

"With a paddy wagon before eight a.m.? When you're rounding up that many people, I guarantee there's a miscarriage of justice somewhere to be found. Sometimes I think they're no better than how they started."

"Stop watching the news with New Nana in the morning. It's got you all riled up," Aunt Ionie grumbled.

Femi picked up a folded piece of paper and squinted. He needed glasses, thick ones, but insisted his contacts worked just fine. "What's all this?"

"Someone wants to buy the house from under us again. Four out of the ten houses on this block have been sold and resold again in the last five years. But since we won't sell, they're trying to prove we don't legally own the house."

Femi and Theo both frowned. That didn't sound good at all. Tatterlys had lived in this same house for well over one hundred years. They've been born inside it and died inside it, and some still haunted it. What would happen to the ghosts? Where would they go? Would Great-Aunt Trudy Anne haunt some new kid? Or what if they don't even have a kid and turn the extra rooms into offices or a home library for their coffee table book collection?

"Fix your faces. This is grown-up business. Don't worry about it," Aunt Cedella chastised.

"This song sounds sad," Theo said, focusing on the music.

"It is sad," she replied, "but if Mahalia can't take you closer to God, I don't know who can."

Chapter 3
The Dungeon

The Dungeon was a CrossFit gym with MMA aspirations on the edge of the Ashley River. It was tucked behind a Kentucky Fried Chicken and a run-down Holiday Inn. A sweaty and mysterious place, it didn't have a parking lot or a sign, and it was attached to a warehouse with blacked-out windows. The only security was an overweight bloodhound and a Catahoula bulldog with cataracts and three legs named Killer. Killer was Theo's favorite. He was always down for a cuddle, even if his breath did smell like he'd been licking his butt all day, because he probably was.

At first glance the place looked like a stand-alone garage, which it was, as its only door could roll up and doubled as one of the walls. The only luxury was a military-style bathroom with three showerheads and a trough urinal. There was one toilet stall, which was so gross Theo had never actually used it. There was a basketball hoop set up on the side of the building, where guys played the kind of streetball you rarely saw outside of New York. A few of the guys were transplants, but most were just b-ball enthusiasts who liked the kind of aggressive play regular gyms don't let you get away with. Sometimes, if he got there early enough, the guys might let him play a game, or if he was really lucky, they might teach him a few moves and drills. He wasn't the only kid who showed up, but he was the most consistent.

Femi barely tapped the brakes to let Theo roll out of the passenger door and onto the sidewalk before he drove away. Theo rehearsed greeting scenarios in his head. Would he give the guys a nod or ask them about what they did in school last week? Maybe it was better if he didn't do anything at all and let them talk to him. Theo's aunts were desperate for him to make friends, but it was hard. Really hard.

On the way to change in the locker room, he walked past the group of Delta Sigma Theta sorority girls from the College of Charleston doing deadlifts in their elephant-print leggings and a pair of surgeons battling it out in a chin lift competition to see whether MUSC or St. Francis Hospital could claim dominance. He quickly snapped a picture for his Instagram and posted it without a caption. He had thousands of followers, but no one knew who he was. He never posted any pics of himself.

When he came out of the locker room, he ran smackdab into Sadhya Elamin, one of Aunt Sabrina's best friends from Siren School, the magical boarding school his aunt told horror stories about. Sadhya was a coowner of the Dungeon with her husband, Raheem. She was short, just barely taller than Theo was, and loved to wear long earrings that dusted her shoulders. She beamed at him. Sadhya Auntie came from a family of Bengali dreamweavers in Bangladesh, and she made more money selling charmed bath oils and salts around the world than she did owning the gym. New Nana swore by her anti-inflammatory bath soaks, saying they were the only thing in the world that helped her arthritis. The warehouse attached to the gym was Sadhya's.

Sadhya Auntie held out her arms and gave Theo a huge hug. He was a little embarrassed that the other guys he balled with could see, but there was no way to stop her, so he just held his arms close to his sides and smiled until she was satisfied.

"There he is!" she sang. She'd majored in mixology at the Magic School in Dubai and was always trying to convince Theo to commit to a career in the magical arts. He hadn't really thought about it too hard.

"What did you bring me?" she asked.

"Hold on." Theo dipped back into the locker room and returned with two gallon jugs of Beauty Water. It was the last of Ro's reserves from a spelunking run she did at Neversink Cave in Alabama. Magic families bartered with each other rather than deal with money. It was their way of keeping connections strong. You had to know what the other needed and trust each other.

Sadhya Auntie clapped her hands together in excitement as he followed her into the warehouse. All of the windows were open, and strawberry finches, lemon-colored orioles, and a few tangerine-breasted starlings flew in and out of the windows. It was Sadhya Auntie's particularly unique magic that attracted songbirds to her, so the air was filled with chirps and the smell of boiling and burning herbs and flowers.

"Do you know how much I need this? It cures almost anything. Acne scars, gone! Cracked nipples from breast-feeding? Poof!"

Theo winced. "Keep your voice down. The guys might hear you," he said, but that only encouraged her, so she launched into a long story about one of her clients who just had twins. Thankfully, Uncle Raheem found them and waved his hands.

"Leave the boy alone. He's here to learn about breaking ankles, not broken skin," he said.

Uncle Raheem was born and raised on Daufuskie Island and had a healing power in his hands, which was useful as a former MMA champion.

Sadyha Auntie waved her hand at him like he was a feral cat begging at her door. "Pah!" She reached down under her sales counter and dropped a gallon-sized plastic bag filled with small black crystals on top. "For you. The proper base for any good warding recipe is kala namak from the salt lakes in Sambhar. Evil eye, curse, hex—none of it can touch you with this. It's like a spiritual brick wall."

Theo put his hand inside the bag and rolled the salt crystals between his forefinger and thumb. They immediately went numb. He smiled. This was high-quality stuff.

"See? You take this but use it sparingly. A little goes a long way."

"Thanks, Auntie!" Theo beamed as he sealed the bag and followed Uncle Raheem into the Dungeon and the smell of sweat, feet, and anguish. He tossed Theo a ball and told him about this fight he'd had with a kid on the island when he was Theo's age.

"He had fists that looked like ham hocks." It was meant to encourage him and get him ready to throw elbows on the court. Killer panted beside him, creating a cloud of dog breath that wrinkled Theo's nose.

"So how's it going?" Uncle Raheem asked as they turned the corner to the asphalt court.

Theo shrugged. Sometimes the words were hard to gather, other times he was fine, but there was something hard-edged about Uncle Raheem. Theo respected him, but he was also a little scared of disappointing him, like maybe the man would crack one of his ribs to make a point. Of course, he had no proof of this, but there was always a first time, wasn't there?

There were only two other kids on the bench, all of them in middle school like Theo. There was Bingo, who had a sleepy eye and no idea that magic existed, and

Leon, whose entire family could charm animals. They owned an exotic pet shop in Mount Pleasant. Leon was taller than both Theo and Bingo, but painfully thin, and Theo sometimes held back when they were matched on the court just to keep from hurting him, but Leon didn't do the same for him.

Too soon Uncle Raheem blew his ref whistle, and Theo was bouncing on the balls of his feet with a mouthguard between his teeth (his aunt insisted).

"Stay loose!" Uncle Raheem shouted. "Hands up!"

Bingo circled him like a beast, but Theo did as he was told. He didn't spring like a panther; he struck like a serpent, quick and efficient. *Lunge, snap, shoot.*

Bingo slipped and scraped his knee twice, but he wasn't fazed, or at least he pretended not to be. He smiled.

"That all you got?" he said.

Theo didn't reply. He circled. Bingo lunged, trying his best at an elbow strike once he had the ball, but missed when he shot and fell forward.

"Hustle!" Uncle Raheem yelled, and Theo faked left and thrust his shoulder into Bingo's chest and then tried an inside leg trip takedown, hoping that if he could make it to the hoop, he could get a rebound. He pictured it in his mind, clear and clean, but it didn't work out that way in real life. He went for the shot and they both stumbled, but Theo ended up on his back. He kicked and popped up within a second, and Bingo was on the ball dribbling slow, so slow Theo saw an opportunity. He struck, his fingers sticky for the rock. Uncle Raheem's voice was in his ears, and then it wasn't. Instead there was a dog—no, a fist—no, an elbow driving toward his left eye.

Uncle Raheem's voice was replaced by a howl. Loud, blinding, and in his head.

Chapter 4

Belly Flop

Aunt Ionie cursed a blue streak when she saw Theo's black eye, but some of Old Nana's bruise cream fixed him right up. Now he smelled like new moon rainwater and goat fat. Instead of the swollen meat biscuit he should be sporting on his face, he'd gotten away with a purple lump the size of a quarter. It still hurt, though. Theo practiced shooting from what he guessed was a three-point line in front of his school. There was a hoop set up on the side of the building for the principal to practice, but he let the students use it sometimes.

"Air ball!" Issa shouted, then bit the head off a Sour Patch Kid. Theo ignored her.

The Robert Smalls School for Excellence was a tiny place. Like other schools, there were teachers, students, computers, and desks, but there were big differences. This school started in the third grade and only went up to the eighth and occupied the first floor of an office building. The second floor was a dentist's office, and the third was some sort of construction company. There wasn't a playground, but there was a park across the street. Most of the kids there hated it, especially Theo's cousin Issa.

Theo shook his head, snatched the ball, and went for a layup.

"Why can't we go to a normal school? I bet you Philip Gray wished he'd gone to a public school instead of that new charter off Cooper Street. Mama said they had, like, five teachers for the entire building, and you had to bring your own lunch. No wonder somebody got snatched," Issa said between bites of gummy body parts. Issa would get possessed by wayward ghosts. She couldn't see them, but they'd hitch a ride in her body whenever she wasn't careful. It was a bum deal in Bikin terms. As a medium, Theo should have conduit abilities, and Issa should be able to see ghosts. They were like two sides of a coin.

"Keep your voice down. Nobody knows where Philip is or what happened to him. You'd have to be psychic to know that," Theo said, reminding her they were incognito. "Besides, you know why we're here. That zoned school building is so full of ghosts I can barely go to the bathroom without someone poking their head into the stall."

"That's gross."

"Yeah, it is. Besides, I like the park."

"You think there'll be a park near the new house if the family gets kicked out?" she asked, as if it weren't the equivalent of asking what would happen if the sun stopped rising.

"The family's not getting kicked out of the house." He said it with finality, like he really believed it, even though a finch flew into his window that morning and everyone knows a bird in the house heralds death. He shooed it out with one of his sketchbooks and locked the window tight. If Great-Aunt Trudy Anne had seen, he knew she'd be making all kinds of fuss, maybe even enough so that someone other than him could see her.

"You can't know what's going to happen. My mom told me a long time ago that there was a charm on the house that kept everybody who wasn't family barred from making changes to it. I guess that would include paperwork and stuff too. If somebody got this far with it, then the charm must have worn off."

"Charms don't wear off. They have to be removed," Theo replied.

"Maybe somebody removed it, then."

"Look. We're not losing the house. I don't wanna talk about it anymore!" Theo huffed.

Issa threw up her hands and mouthed *o-kay*.

Theo looked out at all the kids from his class eating and playing soccer across the street. There was a part of him that wanted to join them, and then there was the bigger part that knew better. No, alone was safer.

His teacher, Mr. Bradley, was talking to someone on his phone. Two ghosts, a man in a top hat and a woman in a long dress, were walking on the path. Theo took a shot, and it bounced off the rim. He rushed to get it.

"Let's go to the fountain," Issa suggested as she picked up the black bean burger in her packed lunch and then put it back. "I want to sing!" she yelled.

"It's what you don't dooooooooooooooooo."

Two girls a few feet away gave her a strange look and then turned their heads. Issa frowned.

"What are you looking at?" she spat.

The girl on the right had frizzy Afro puffs and really wet lips from too much lip gloss. She rolled her neck and stood up.

"I don't know, what am I looking at? Don't start nothin', and it won't be nothin'!" the girl yelled.

The girl on the right pulled her friend down so that her butt plopped on the bench. She then gave Theo a weak smile as she whispered something in the other girl's ear. They turned around.

"Don't do that," Theo said to Issa. While he avoided trouble, Issa was more likely to drop-kick it in the chest and then ask him to back her up.

"They gave *me* funny looks. I've been on my best behavior since school started, I swear. Even though I can *feel* the ghosts calling so bad that my stomach is in knots, I haven't had one possession in front of anybody," Issa whined. "These kids are just boring. Rejects from the zoned school."

"You mean like us?" he said and took another shot. It bounced, then circled the rim, but made it in.

"None of them like to dance or sing or do anything fun. They just want to sit and stare and try not to sweat."

Robert Smalls was a small school for kids who wanted to start their own businesses—really just kids of parents who want their kids to grow up and start their own businesses. Issa wanted to go to a school for the performing arts, but her parents nixed that idea.

"Come on. We can go over to that fountain." Theo pointed to a corner of the park with a small fountain that had a statue of a girl dancing in the center. Issa shook her head.

"Are there fish in it?" she asked.

"I don't think so," he answered.

"Well, then, the aquarium it is!" she yelled, and in a blink she was running toward the city bus.

Issa was slightly older than Theo, but it was his job to take care of her. She had a habit of running around the city, and with her particular gift she could be trouble. Big trouble.

"How did you convince me to do this?" Theo asked as he gazed out of the windows of the city bus.

"'Cause you were just as bored as I was. Bet you got a knot in your stomach too," she said, and he didn't want to admit that after missing his chance with Billy at the park the other day he hadn't been himself. He went back once and waited, but Billy didn't show. He hated how the magic called to him, ached for him to use it, but not more than he hated that Issa could smell it on him.

"Don't worry. You don't have to answer. I already know."

Issa pulled the string on the bus so they could be let off at the Charleston Harbor. The aquarium sat on the edge of the water in a big gray and glass building. There was a giant digital billboard showing the new deep ocean animal exhibit with a neon picture of a jellyfish flashing prettily high above the roof. It quickly changed to a picture of Philip Gray. Theo looked away. He noticed Issa was getting farther ahead of him, so he ran to catch up.

They passed a row of construction vehicles, yet nothing was being built or removed. The walkway went through a huge fish tank, and sea turtles, sharks, and seahorses swam above their heads as they walked in. Theo had to admit that this was a lot better than listening to Bianca Manifort explain why chocolate chip cookies would sell better than sugar cookies at the school bake sale.

"*We are unstoooooooooppaaaaaaaaable,*" Issa sang.

The other visitors looked in her direction, but it was the fish who really stood up and paid attention. As she sang, they all swam toward where she stood closest to the glass.

"She's special, that one," said a man with an Australian accent. Theo didn't turn around. He knew it was a ghost, and he didn't want anyone thinking he was talking to himself. He put his earbuds in and walked over to Issa to stand close to her.

"Do you work here?" Theo asked the man as the ghost came to stand next to him. He looked younger than Aunt Ionie, but not by much. His hair was red, and he wore baggy shorts and tan boots. He hadn't been dead long, because Theo could see right through him. Older ghosts were more powerful; they almost looked like real people.

The ghost nodded. "Name's Roddy. I'm a marine biologist. I only worked here three months before the accident."

"Is it nice here?" Theo asked.

"It is. I like the animals, and I can meet people. Like you, like her."

Theo looked up at the ghost. "Don't touch her. Don't even talk to her."

"Hey, hey! Don't get touchy. I'm just making conversation."

People around Theo and Issa began to stare. She was singing some old Celia Cruz song that was making the sea turtles sing back in their weird turtle voices. They were causing a scene. Theo pulled Issa's arm and led them out of the tunnel.

"Hey, I was having fun."

"I know. We're being watched," Theo reminded her.

Issa smiled and straightened her shoulders. She didn't mind being watched; in fact, she liked it very much.

"There are ghosts here."

Issa frowned. "There are ghosts everywhere. Why would here be any different?"

Theo frowned back. "Do you have any salt in your bag?"

She shook her head.

"Brick dust?"

She shook her head again. Aunt Ionie had tried to make her a talisman, but anything you put against her skin made her break out in hives.

"How are you supposed to keep ghosts away if you charm fish and let everyone in here know you're a medium?"

He was angry, and he didn't hide it.

"I'm not a medium. You are. I'm just a conduit, and if the fish like my singing, I can't help that. Besides, I got some of Aunt Sabrina's activator in here." She pulled a small blue and white bottle whose original brand name had been rubbed off, but still had *activator* spelled out on the side. "Pure ghost poison. Psalm 91 ash, coconut water, and rose oil." She then spritzed herself like it was perfume.

"Ain't that supposed to be for Jheri curls?" an older lady mumbled, and Theo moved them farther away. "That stuff'll give you pimples, baby girl," they heard the lady say.

Issa rolled her eyes. "I got some Everflame in here too. I've never tried it before, though. Mama says you can set yourself on fire if you aren't careful." She pulled out a can of hair spray that looked older than the activator bottle, then put it back.

"And what about the ghosts who know you're a conduit and are just waiting for you to slip up? What's the expiration date on that, anyway?"

She shrugged. Once an opera singer slipped into Issa's skin and sang for seven straight hours, until her voice gave out. Issa wasn't able to talk for nearly a week. She could never see the ghosts, but Theo could. After the opera incident, he'd been assigned to keep her safe while they were at school. It was the main reason Issa had been transferred.

"You know what? You're no fun."

"You're no fun either. I don't want to have to babysit you. I could be in science class right now. We were getting to the astronomy unit. I like astronomy!" he barked. That was a lie.

Issa's eyes narrowed, and she poked Theo in the chest with her bony finger.

"You don't babysit me. I'm older than you by six months. I babysit you, Snot Boy!!"

Chapter 5
A Song for Turtles

The aquarium visitors gave Theo a wide berth, but between the shrieks of glee from toddlers breaking away from their mothers and the overzealous barks from school trip chaperones, he didn't warrant that much attention.

"She's a bit of a hothead," Roddy announced, regarding Issa's antics. "She reminds me of this pirate that sometimes shows up around here. She took over her husband's ship after he fell overboard and was eaten by sharks. She laughed when she told me that story. Can you believe that? Laughing at your husband's grisly death? Anyway, that girl you came with reminds me of her. They've got the same fiery eyes. I never knew her name. She liked to behead the visitors with her scabbard. Didn't work, though sometimes it'd make their necks itch. She liked that. Best to keep your distance."

"Go away," Theo said. He'd forgotten about the marine biologist and really just wanted to be alone. He was staring at an albino alligator. Roddy walked through the glass to stand opposite him and blocked his view.

"I'm a good listener, you know."

Theo took a step to the right so he wouldn't have to stare into the man's misty belly. "Most ghosts are great listeners," Theo replied and hit Play on his phone. It was some playlist Frank had shared with him: Toosii, Tobe Nwigwe, and some guy from Belgium who rapped all in French. He could still hear Roddy talking, but Roddy didn't know that, so he just stood there.

Theo thought about leaving Issa at the aquarium. Everyone assumed they were on a field trip, so they wouldn't be bothered while they were inside, but someone might notice if he left on his own, and then what would happen to Issa? His aunties would hit the roof if they found out he'd left her by herself. Why was he the one to have to take care of her? Why did he have to listen to the dead and their stories?

Someone pulled on his shoulder. He looked down. The girl couldn't have been any older than four. She wore a sailor suit and a big white bow in her hair. Her skin was pale but not translucent and even though she was moving her mouth he couldn't understand a word she was saying. He pulled out his earbuds.

"It's Portuguese," Roddy offered from inside the exhibit.

Theo knelt down so that he was at her level and held up his earbud so she could listen to the music. She smiled.

"You lost?" he asked. She looked at him, confused. He then noticed that her eyes were cloudy.

Theo turned to Roddy. "Can you translate?"

"Oh, so now you want to talk to me?" Roddy snorted.

"Can you help or not?" Theo asked. The ghost nodded.

"Você está perdida?"

The girl nodded. Theo smiled at her and stood, stuffing his earbuds into his pocket. He held out his hand to her, and she took it. She'd been dead so long, it felt almost solid.

"Where are you taking her?" Roddy asked.

"To find her gateway," Theo replied and pulled out his teetotum from his backpack. It looked like a dreidel, but this one had adinkra on its six sides. He'd use it to lead him to the best portal site nearby, but spinning it in front of people could cause a scene, so he just palmed it in case he needed it.

"But she can't leave the harbor. She's been here longer than I have. If she hasn't found it by now . . ."

Theo ignored him and then tried to ignore the people who gave him weird looks as he made his way out of the exhibit hall, holding the hand of an invisible girl.

"We're going to find Issa."

Theo listened for the singing. The sound echoed and bounced off the walls, and he followed it. He found her at the sea turtle exhibit, singing to them.

"She's amazing," one of the staff commented. "I've never seen them respond like that to anyone."

Theo knew that was probably true. He waited for her to finish her song and then walked over to her. She stood and stared at him with a funny look in her eye, like he was a stranger. He knew that he wasn't looking at his cousin then, but someone else. Still holding the little girl's hand, he reached into his pocket and covered his hand with a bit of brick dust.

"Issa?" he asked just to be sure.

When she didn't respond, he very quickly and very firmly smacked her in the chest, palm up and fingers curled. She flew back a bit and whoever had slipped into Issa's body was knocked clear. The spirit was old and stumbled just like Issa did.

"Hey!" it protested. It was a tall woman with red hair and in an equally red dress and heels. She looked angry. "What did you do that for?"

Theo stared back angrily as he ignored the other people at the aquarium who weren't too happy he'd just hit a girl.

"You have to ask permission before taking over someone's body."

The spirit snarled. "I did ask. She didn't say nothin'!"

"She can't see you," he spat and led the little girl over to his cousin.

A teacher from another school was rubbing Issa's back. People were staring at him like he was dangerous. All eyes were on him, and it felt like his skin was covered in bugs. Nothing good comes from stares.

He knelt down in front of Issa. "Are you okay?" he asked.

"Where is your teacher?" the woman asked firmly.

"We're homeschooled. He's my brother," Issa managed to squeak out. The teacher frowned.

"Well, where are your parents, then?" she asked. "There is no excuse to hit a girl."

Theo could see that she wasn't going to let this go, and they only had a few more moments before the teacher called a security guard over or sent one of her students to do it for her. Theo raised his eyebrows at Issa. This was her cue to do something. They needed a distraction. They needed to get away.

She sighed heavily. "Oh, all right."

She turned toward the turtle tank and knelt down so her head was as close to the water as possible and then whispered something that neither he nor the teacher standing next to them could hear. Sometimes—not always—Issa could suggest something to an animal, and they'd respond. She insisted it wasn't a true power, but some weird leftover fluke from a Bikin ghost who took over her body once in preschool.

Just then, every turtle, even those who had just started playing a game of pop your head out of the water, stopped moving. Then, one by one, they crawled out of the tank, and began to walk down the hallway. Everyone except Issa and Theo followed, even the teacher who wasn't as into the turtles as the horde of kids she had to monitor.

He sat down next to his cousin, his white jeans getting just a bit wet as he waited for her to sit up.

"Why'd you let that lady in?"

"You know I can't see them," Issa said with a pout.

"Yes, but she said she asked you. I know you can hear them, at least sometimes."

She avoided his eyes and looked around at the exhibit walls covered in diagrams of every species of turtle.

"I like it, okay? It makes me feel powerful, and I don't mind what they do. They won't hurt me. I'm them. They want to stay as long as they can."

"But they could hurt you if they wanted."

"You sound just like your old aunties. None of you like to have any f—"

Issa's voice cut off, and her head swiveled in the direction of the hallway. Theo's head did the same. They had both heard the scream. It wasn't the kind of thing you heard every day. It wasn't the kind of scream people made. It was the kind ghosts made. The little ghost girl waved her hand in front of Theo's face so he could see her. He'd almost forgotten she was there. She looked scared. Worse than that, she looked terrified.

"We need to go." Theo grabbed his cousin's hand and pulled, but she stood firm.

The screams grew louder and the ground rumbled under his feet. "Do you feel that?" she asked.

He did. But he felt like lead was in his shoes. There were spirits here. Angry spirits, sad ones. More than he'd sensed when they arrived. It was like they must have been hiding. Something crashed down the hall.

"We need to go now!" he said, not raising his voice but deepening it.

Again, Issa shook her head. Just then a stampede of people ran past the exhibit toward what looked like the nearest exit. The lights began to flicker. The ghost screams grew louder. He wouldn't leave Issa—he'd never do that, even though he might think about it—but what he did might just have been worse.

With one quick and powerful shove, he pushed the little ghost girl into the body of Issa.

Chapter 6
The Hag

Theo grabbed Issa's—well, the ghost girl's hand—and peeked into the hallway, but she snatched it away, gazing wide-eyed at her own hands, flexing the fingers for a moment and then jumping up and down before she poked him in the ribs.

"Ow!" Theo hissed.

She laughed and seemed to be even more taken by the sound it made, so she laughed again.

"Okay. Get ahold of yourself. You're borrowing a body, but we have bigger problems."

"O que?" she questioned and then began babbling in Portuguese, none of which Theo could understand. He pressed his hand against her mouth.

"Shhh!" he said, and then pointed to his ears, hoping she understood that they needed to be quiet. She nodded and let him grab her hand again before they both peeped around the corner.

There they saw her, the hag. Her mouth gaped open, wide as a beach ball, and her lips curled back from her teeth so that her black gums peeked out like seaweed. Green tears, thick and slick as snot, streaked down her gray cheeks, and she tottered from side to side, looking but not seeing. Her stick-thin arms reached in every direction, trying to touch something or someone, but they never rested.

"She's the nanny," Roddy said to Theo, suddenly appearing at his side again.

"But this is an aquarium."

"That's what the children call her."

"Ela os ama até a morte," the ghost girl whispered.

Roddy translated: "She says the hag loves the children to death. Gruesome."

The hag startled and tried to straighten her skeletal frame. She closed her gaping mouth for just a moment, and Theo and his ghost crew could see what she must have looked like long ago. Thin, painfully so, in a ribboned and corseted dress with tattered and scraggly lace at the bottom. It may have been blue at one time, but all of its color had been washed away. Now, it was rotted in some places, moldy in others, but soaking wet all over. It dripped like a broken faucet with each of her steps. She sniffed the air like a dog catching a scent. Theo nearly tripped over his sneakers as he backed away slowly, pulling Issa along with him—but she wasn't Issa, she was a little girl who'd been terrorized by this creature for who knows how long. She wouldn't move, she was so frozen by fear. He pulled on her elbow and caught her reflection in the glass of the shark tank. Her eyes were wide and pleading, and he could see Issa's face and the ghost girl's face fighting for who would control their combined bodies.

"C'mon," Theo whispered as he tried again to get her to move, but she didn't hear him. All she saw was walking death headed her way, and she looked too scared to move. She turned to him and released a flurry of Portuguese that even Roddy seemed confused by.

"I don't know. Something about a dog, I think, and a man in tall boots. It doesn't make any sense," he said.

Theo moved to pick her up so they could get moving fast, and a sliver of panic caused her to scream. It was just loud enough for the hag to know which direction to head, and once she knew, her wobbling, crick-cracking steps turned into a run.

"We gotta go!" Theo shouted. In the tug-of-war between the ghost girl and his cousin, Issa won out and expelled the ghost girl, just in time for Issa and Theo to hightail it toward the exit and the ghost girl to dissolve into the shark tank to hide.

Theo's backpack slammed into his back and felt like it weighed a hundred pounds as they ran, but he'd never run so fast in his life, making sure to hold Issa's hand.

They crashed into the locked exit doors.

"We're trapped!" Issa screamed as the hag came ever closer.

Roddy's ghostly face was twisted in worry, and his chest heaved, though he'd long given up the need to breathe. "There's an emergency exit, down that hall." He pointed. "It leads up onto the street. Go!"

Theo ran, but he knew they wouldn't make it. He slipped one shoulder strap off as he ran and dug into the front pocket of his backpack. He grabbed a sandwich bag full of an experimental warding recipe of brick dust, Tellicherry black peppercorns, rock salt, and crushed alligator bone. It slowed him down.

Issa crashed into the emergency exit, but the door was too heavy to open herself.

"Help me!" she yelled.

The hag let out an excited screech, close as she was to her prey. In long strides she covered twice the distance Theo and Issa could with one step, and like the winner of a deadly race, she stretched out her arms to claim her prize.

But Theo already had his right hand full of his warding salt and his back pressed against the door.

"Not today," he said as he tossed the salt into her twisted face. She wailed as she was knocked off her feet. She flew back so fast that she slammed into the shark tank, cracking the glass. Then something howled in the distance.

"How did she do that?!" Theo shouted, shocked. Ghosts could scare, haunt, maybe rattle a doorknob, but break glass? That's a spirit with the kind of power Theo had never seen before.

In seconds, she was gone, and the crack turned into a gash, sending rushing water and sea animals into the hallway and up the stairs to the street, soaking Theo and Issa as they made their escape.

Chapter 7
The Night Market

It was nearly seven o'clock when Theo and Issa crossed the threshold of the Tatterly home, soaked to the bone and smelling like fish guts.

Aunt Ionie saw them first.

"Let me explain," Theo said, as he held his hands up in surrender.

Aunt Ionie didn't even say a word, she just shook her head and buzzed, like a honeybee. It was a thing she did when she wanted you to shut your mouth and shut it immediately. Her eyes raked over them both, checking for missing fingers, broken skin, or blood. Finding none, she finally stood back, her shadow towering over them, as she was quite tall.

"Now. Explain to me how two underaged Bikin such as yourselves found your way to the aquarium alone, without a teacher, without a parent, without anyone who could look after you at all and for so long a time as it would make you slosh in here past dinnertime."

"I . . ." Issa started, but Aunt Ionie, her eyes as big as golf balls, buzzed again.

"Then explain to me how two scions of the Tatterly name such as yourselves managed to level an entire aquarium, knowing full well that your family would find out, knowing full well the consequences of sneaking out, knowing full well that you might be seen by other Bikin and that those Bikin would undoubtedly call one of your many aunties and tell them they had seen your little disobedient selves gallivanting downtown without a care in the world! Hmmm? Answer me when I'm talking to you!"

"Aunt Ionie . . ." Theo started again, but she buzzed even louder this time, getting nose to nose with them both.

"I don't want to hear anything from either of you."

"But . . ."

"You heard me! I won't have any backtalk in my house. Strip off those filthy clothes and take a shower. Both of you!"

Theo and Issa stripped off their shoes at the door and trudged to the laundry room to dump their clothes. Theo let Issa go in first so she could wrap herself in a towel.

"Whew! You guys smell like rotten eggs and chitlins," Femi exclaimed, his ubiquitous bowl of Cocoa Crispers in hand as he walked down the hallway. "Got yourselves into a bit of trouble, did you?"

"Shut up."

"Don't you even want to know what the aunties plan to do with you?"

"Of course I do, but I ain't gonna beg you for details. I'm too tired," Theo said, and then he immediately yawned. He sagged against the laundry room door, praying for Issa to hurry up so he could go upstairs, take a hot shower in some eucalyptus soap, and collapse into bed. Sure, he was hungry too, but that would mean facing off with the aunties, and he wasn't about to volunteer for that. Both his belly and his punishment could wait until the morning.

"Well, you're lucky I'm in a generous mood tonight," Femi said. At that moment Issa opened the door.

"Oh really?" she said. "C'mon, then."

"You are gonna stay here for the weekend," he said to her. She shrugged.

"So what? I stay here all the time," she replied.

"Aunt Sabrina had a vision. She's been painting all day. Don't ask, 'cause I don't know what it is. It's some big secret. Aunt Cedella's gonna take you both to see Granddad at the Night Market."

Theo and Issa both groaned at the same time. Femi snickered as he chewed another mouthful of his Crispers.

"Are you sure?" Theo asked.

Femi nodded. "I just overheard her on the phone. You guys are going for a reading and who knows how many hours of service."

Theo dropped his head back against the wall, wishing he could just disappear. Seeing Granddad wasn't bad. He loved Granddad, who always told great stories, but he hated getting readings, and he hated service. The readings were fine for other people, but Theo was a medium. All they ever saw was death—his death, the death of whoever was in the room, and all the possible deaths that might occur over the next few weeks. Still, there were little tidbits here and there that could be useful.

Aunt Cedella swore by a good reading when things weren't absolutely normal and boring at home. As for service, that was the worst part. It could be anything, like setting traps in the surrounding marsh for tikiloshes and nincis, gremlin-like creatures that can turn invisible and like to cause trouble at the best of times. At the worst of times they can be downright deadly. Or Theo and Issa might be roped into babysitting in the play area where everyone drops their toddlers so they can shop.

Theo's phone buzzed with a missed call from his mom. His stomach flipped. Normally, he'd be upset that he'd missed her since her service wasn't so great in her digs, but this time all he could feel was relief. He'd get at least one more day to come up with a good excuse as to why he'd gotten in trouble.

Theo looked up from his phone and back to Femi. "And where are you gonna be? I don't see how Aunt Cedella is gonna let an educational trip to the Night Market go to waste on her favorite nephew."

Femi snorted. "First off, I'm not her favorite. No one is. And don't worry where I'll be. I've got really important junior year stuff to worry about, so whatever I'm doing it's going to be ten times more interesting and less tiring than whatever you guys are doing. Sleep tight. Don't let the nincis bite!"

The Night Market was old, as old as Charleston itself, in that it began as just an old stump where enslaved people gathered to speak their own languages, play songs from their homelands, and then eventually practice their own magic. Now, it was more village than market, with people who lived there full time. Most of the activities didn't even happen at night, so the name was just silly now. But still that same feeling of peace and freedom and excitement was there whenever anyone crossed the threshold from the ordinary world into the extraordinary world of the market.

Theo and Issa walked beside Aunt Cedella in matching wading boots. She'd spent half an hour in the attic searching for a pair with the right kind of adjustable shoulder straps to fit Theo's and Issa's small bodies. They looked like they were about to compete in the middle school category at a fly fishing competition; instead they were sulking as they waddled in their large fishing boots behind their aunt, dreading their service assignment.

"But, Auntie, don't you think I'm more suited to working in the baby room? Those bags of ninci repellant are really heavy, and really, what would people think? The Tatterlys sending such a little girl off to do such a big job. It doesn't look right."

Aunt Cedella sucked her teeth.

"Keep talking and you'll be right back here next weekend. You can't even watch yourself, now you're talkin' 'bout watchin' somebody else's baby. Chile, please."

"Let it go," Theo mumbled as they waddled. Issa was right, though: the other people walking through the trees were looking at them. Some of them snickered; others shook their heads in pity. They knew what the kids were in for, and they also knew it was probably a punishment. Next to nobody wanted to work in the marsh.

To get to the market it took a little time and even more memory, because there weren't any roads. People usually had their own special spots where they pulled off Highway 17 onto a dirt road so narrow a pickup truck couldn't fit, and even if it did the brush and branches reached too low for it to make it through. Then you had to pull off the dirt road to walk and then walk some more until the tree line gave way to miles of sandflats, creeks, shrunken islands, and pluff mud that stretched to the horizon.

On good days you could see nothing but herons and seagulls snapping up blue crab and grass shrimp in thickets of cordgrass. On those days the water might be low enough to see diamondback turtles or the occasional otter floating on its back or peeping its head up to see why you were headed out in a kayak at the crack of dawn with your stern-faced aunt and spitting mad cousin, who needed to just chill out so you could get through the day. But it wasn't one of those sunny days. Instead it was hot and drizzly. The mosquitoes hovered in hazy black swarms, and even though Aunt Cedella affixed a guiding stone to the front of the boat the trip felt like it was taking longer than usual.

The three cut through miles of spartina and black needlerush with just a skiff and a pole to navigate through the sandy mix of saltwater and freshwater until the Night Market's island appeared behind a burst of marsh hens erupting into the air. At first glance it looked just like a tiny island of trees above the water line, but for those who could really see, it was a small city pulsing with magical energy. Their tiny boat docked, and Aunt Cedella pulled the small thing up on the shore and turned it over next to someone else's. She pointed her bony finger at them both and squinted her heavily made-up eyes. Aunt Cedella was a little heavy-handed with the eyeliner. She looked kind of like an Egyptian hieroglyphic, a fact she'd been told more than once, but she took it as a compliment.

"So here's how this is gonna go. You two are going to spend the entire morning with Queen Chet."

Both Issa and Theo moaned in anticipated agony.

"She's the worst, Auntie!" Theo objected.

Aunt Cedella snapped her fingers to stop their collective nonsense. "You shoulda thought about that before you leveled the aquarium."

"But that wasn't our fault," Theo argued. "We were being chased by the . . ."

Aunt Cedella snapped her fingers again.

"I don't want to hear it. You will be hardworking and respectful, and if Queen sends me anything but glowing reviews of your work, you will be knee-deep in Bili ape scat for the next six months, I swear to God!"

Issa and Theo looked at each other and threw away any thoughts of objecting. The only thing worse than ninci duty was cleaning out the Bili ape cages in the animal enclosures.

"All right! I see that got your attention. After your selfless and dedicated service to the Bikin community, you may peruse the market for lunch before meeting me for your reading appointment at one o'clock. What time?"

Issa and Theo replied in unison, "One o'clock."

The entrance to the Night Market is a wide wrought iron gate under a wooded archway of willow branches, wild cherry, and braided sweetgrass, flanked on each side by swamp cyrilla shrubs so thick it was like a wall. As soon as Theo walked through the gate, he could smell the oysters frying somewhere deep in the center of the market at his favorite food stall, but he'd have to wait.

"I'll check you guys in, and from then until Queen Chet releases you, you're nothing but God's angels sent down from heaven. Got me?"

"Yes ma'am," they both chimed.

Queen Chet towered over them in a pair of duck boots. Her gray dreadlocks were piled on top of her head like an upturned bowl of spaghetti. She smiled, a gold tooth glinting from the back of her mouth.

"Ready for some hard work?"

Chapter 8
Ninci Duty

Queen Chet sloshed through the marsh with a machete in hand, chopping down sawgrass with great wide swats of her arm. A hand-rolled cigar dangled from her lips, and sweet smoke wafted behind her, which made Issa sneeze and burned Theo's nostrils, but they followed close behind. Queen Chet was the master of the marsh, and they had no intention of getting lost or left behind.

"Do you know how nincis came to be?" she asked.

"No ma'am," Theo replied as he dodged the tip of her machete blade.

"They're ocean pests. Scavengers who liked to pick the bones of pirates who were thrown overboard."

"I thought those were mermaids," Issa interrupted.

"Hush, girl. Didn't your mama teach you anything at all? Mermaids are just Mama Wati's sisters. Nincis are blood-sucking, air-breathing water monsters with the bodies of otters and the head of a lobster. They live in nests and overwhelm their prey in sheer numbers, crawling over them en masse and eating them alive."

Theo winced.

"Nincis are the result of bitter magic, a mistake someone not too much older than you made when they tried to fix a problem on their own instead of asking for help. Hunting like this used to be a family thing. A ritual done every new moon by the first families. Not all of them, but a representative. I used to love it when it was all girls. We'd bring all kinds of explosives and have us a time."

Theo wanted to say that he often asked for help, but the adults were always too busy or told him to hush and go do his homework or something else instead of listening, but he didn't think Queen Chet would listen either, so he kept his thoughts to himself.

"Why'd they stop?" Issa asked.

"There were twelve first families. The Tatterlys, Mortons, Carols, you know. They founded the Night Market. This was the heart of our power and our refuge, and to some extent it still is, but folks like to talk about all the stuff we gained after integration without talking about the stuff we lost. Before the civil rights movement, we couldn't eat at the same lunch counters as the white citizens of Charleston, and we couldn't go to the same schools, but we had our own restaurants and schools with teachers who cared and waitstaff who asked after your sick nana. Once integration came, we could go anywhere, but those white folks didn't go to our restaurants, so they closed, and those teachers who loved us so much couldn't find jobs in the integrated schools. I say all this to say that after things opened up, the families started to drift apart and spread out, and our power began to thin and fade. We didn't have enough people to do the hunts, so they stopped."

"So we used to be more powerful than we are now? I didn't know that," Theo said.

Queen Chet shook her head. "Silly child. We ain't gone just sit idly by and let our power die. The heads of the families created amplifiers. It's a charm linked to your family blood. The ancestors used to use them to connect to their people at home in Africa across the ocean. Your children could be separated from you or you from any other Bikin. The amplifiers made it possible for the magic in the blood to sing no matter where a child was, or if there was anyone there to teach them. We didn't use them for a long time, 'cause we didn't need them, but that's why it's important to know your history. You might need those old charms one day. The families set them amplifiers down here and linked them so they'd be stronger. Each family is connected to the other, and that provides a sort of protection. Magic is in your blood, but there's a family failsafe too. This land. Your house. The Carols worked with sculpture, and they got pieces at the Gibbes Museum downtown. The Rileys are so secretive no one knows what their amplifier is or where."

Theo thought about that and swallowed hard. His house was more important than he thought.

"What would happen if one of the amplifiers were destroyed or lost?" he asked.

Queen Chet stopped short and stood stock-still, as if she were a tiger about to pounce, but then relaxed her muscles and kept walking. "The amplifiers are linked to all of us, so if one falls, so do we all. We'd be vulnerable. There's a debate going on with some of the old members who believe that the amplifiers are more trouble than they worth 'cause they attract demons. Some believe it and others don't. I think it's unique to each family. Everybody got their own history. Once a family's magic amplifies, it could call out for a balance in energy, a counterweight. Demons with an agenda might feel compelled to make an attack. But like I said, it's just a theory."

They were far from the Night Market, and the grass had grown so far over their heads that the sun was blocked out. Queen Chet puffed on her cigar a little harder and slowed down.

"There's a nest somewhere here. Take out those flares I gave you. You light 'em when I tell you to. Now put those goggles on and keep your mouth shut. Did I tell you nincis spit poison?"

"No," Theo croaked, his voice breaking with just the tiniest bit of fear.

"Sorry 'bout that. Keep your mouth shut, like I said. If one crawls up your leg, smack it between the eyes with your fist and stick those earplugs in, 'cause they've got a helluva scream."

Queen Chet was just finished with her rules of engagement when Theo heard the rattle. He turned to his right and saw the grass shift in a way that could only be an animal.

"Earplugs in, kids," Queen Chet whispered, and then she took a swipe at the grass. A chunk of the natural wall fell like snipped hair and revealed two beady eyes, like black gumballs peeking up through the clippings. They blinked once and looked at Queen Chet and then to Theo. Nobody moved.

"Now!" Queen Chet yelled, but Theo could only see her mouth move. And then the sky turned blue-black as nincis erupted from the brush. In a breath he was covered in no less than twelve wriggling and pinching nincis.

He howled as a ninci grabbed hold of his thumb and ear, but he lit his flare just as Queen Chet showed him and turned to Issa, who for all her girly tendencies was punching the little buggers right between the eyes with all her might. She barely had a scratch on her.

Jab! Jab! Jab! She was like Gervonta Davis in earrings.

As soon as his green flare erupted they scattered, but Queen Chet waved Theo and Issa on with her machete so they could follow the nincis into their nest. Theo pulled at his throbbing ear as he followed, and it didn't take long to find the nest, a green bulge of mud and grass that looked like a pimple waiting to be popped.

Queen Chet holstered her machete and dug into her right boot to pull out what looked like three saltshakers.

She tossed one to Theo and the other to Issa, and they all began to shake out the contents around the mound.

Theo wrinkled his nose as the smell of rotting fish and dead meat filled the air. At a closer look he could see that the top of the mound wasn't made of just grass, but also bones and decaying birds. He threw up a little in his mouth. Something not yet dead twitched atop the mound as Queen Chet shook out the last of her potion onto the tiny hill and then flicked her cigar onto the pile.

It exploded in the brightest, highest fire Theo had ever seen. It was like hell had opened its mouth, or a tiny volcano had decided to erupt for exactly one minute, and then it was over. A black crater had been scooped out of the earth and was quickly filling with seawater.

Queen Chet smiled wide, her dreadlocks and goggles a mess of green ninci guts. She slipped off the goggles and bent to wash them clean in the water, and Theo pulled out his earplugs.

"Well! That was fun, now wasn't it?" Queen Chet said.

Theo leaned toward Issa as he pulled off his wading boots.

"Want to hear a joke?" he asked her.

She rolled her eyes as she used a hand towel to wipe the muck from her neck. She pulled away a mucus-covered mandible the size of a small comb. She dry heaved, then caught herself. They both tossed the shower caps Queen Chet had given them earlier, thankful that they had listened to their aunt and just did what they were told and didn't ask questions.

"Fine. What's the joke? And it better be funny."

"Why did the ninci cross the road?"

She rolled her eyes again as she hopped on one foot to get the other duck boot off. "Why?"

"To get to the side Queen Chet isn't lacing with powder bombs to annihilate your entire family."

Issa snorted. "Okay. It was kinda funny."

"You kids handled yourselves pretty well this morning. Nobody puked. You've still got all your fingers. You should be proud you performed so well for your community. I know this detail isn't the easiest in the list of service activities."

Theo's smile was wobbly and insincere, but he tried. "It was our pleasure, Queen Chet."

"Good. Good. I'll be sure to tell your aunt how much I enjoyed you both. Maybe you'll come back and help me hunt some tikoloshes next time. I'll teach you how to use a heat-seeking bow and arrow. My own design. The trick is to put some chimera tears into your tip covering. I'll show you next time. We've had some of the trackers come back with a few leads."

"Sounds like fun," Issa said, her voice rising on the end as she lied. "Is there somewhere we can clean up a bit more?"

"Sure! I've got a little station here around back. I've also got a wicking spell that works pretty well."

She opened a large chest and pulled out a beautifully feathered fan and a thumb of incense.

"You know, the peacocks and peahens that roam around here are said to be the reincarnated spirits of the escaped enslaved people who hid in these marshes. It's a privilege for them to give up one of their feathers. They have power. A visiting shaman from João Pessoa blessed this one for me. He came from a family of fishermen. Pretty useful if you don't want to smell like fish guts all day."

She lit the thumb of incense in a small clay bowl and then wafted the smoke over them both with the fan in a flutter. Immediately, every bit of moisture blew off them in the breeze.

Issa was so grateful that she hugged Queen Chet, which surprised them both.

Queen Chet patted her back awkwardly. "Well, you're . . . uh . . . welcome. Go get something to eat. Tell them it's on me, and make sure you go see the forest bull at the zoo enclosure."

Refreshed, Theo and Issa went in search of food. On the way, he checked his phone for a message from his mom, but there wasn't anything new. She'd left a super-long voice note about the importance of obedience. He'd replied with one word. *Okay.*

"Oysters! Oysters! Oysters!" Theo chanted and tried to get Issa to join him.

"I'm a vegetarian now."

"Since when?" he asked, surprised.

"Since yesterday," she chirped brightly. "Mama says that spirits won't be so attracted to me if I stop consuming dead animals."

Theo laughed until his stomach ached. "Are you kidding me? Now it is my personal mission to make you break."

"You can't make me break. I'm immune to peer pressure."

"Nobody's immune to peer pressure."

"I am. Always have been. Aunt Ionie says I have a particularly strong will."

"Yeah, she says that when she wants to call you a brat but doesn't want to hurt your feelings."

"That's not fair."

"It isn't." He stopped walking in the middle of the road and looked at her. "Why couldn't you just have gone home on Friday?"

"Who told you to follow me? You're not my father or my warden. I can do whatever I want. Admit it. Your life would be outrageously boring without me."

"Issa. I see ghosts. My life is anything but boring."

"Forget all that. So what? You see ghosts. I'm talking about fun. You wouldn't have any fun if it wasn't for little old me. You'd be stuck in that house talking to Great-Aunt Trudy Anne all weekend. What do you guys do, anyway? Play board games? I mean, do you even have any friends besides me? And honestly, I don't even count, because I'm family."

Issa started walking faster, so she couldn't hear Theo's reply, but he didn't care. What did she know about his life? It was fine. Totally fine. He had friends. There was

Brian . . . well, no, that kid moved away, and they really only had played basketball a few times after school. But there were also the Rollins twins, though they weren't really friends since they only hung out to complete that science project, and Theo didn't really feel comfortable with them in the house since the ghosts would feel a way about him ignoring them while his friends were there. He really did only hang around family. His shoulders slumped as he realized that Issa, the pain that she was, really was his one and only *true* friend.

He caught up with her.

"So what are you gonna eat, anyway?" he asked.

She didn't reply immediately but eventually broke once they made their way down the cobblestone path to the food stall quarter. On each side of the narrow path stalls were selling medicines and tasty delights, some with magical aftereffects, and some just delicious. Theo and Issa walked up to Theo's favorite stall, Mister P. Patterson's Po' Boys. The stall jutted out into the street via a tiny wooden gate, but the top was just a tri-colored tent with a sign that looked like it had been there for a hundred years. There were a few patrons sitting at the bistro tables, but they didn't pay any attention to two kids.

"What can I get ya?" Mister P. asked as Theo approached the counter. He didn't even have to look at the chalkboard menu to know what he wanted. It's what he always got when he came.

"One oyster po' boy, extra pickle, extra Patterson sauce, with a side of kettle chips with yumboe dust. Oh, and a large fizzy lemon. Queen Chet said to put it on her tab."

Mister P., a short, squat man with almond skin and a coarse red Afro, laughed. "So Queen sent you, huh? I guess you two got good and dirty this morning?"

Theo shrugged.

"All right then. Anything for you, sweetheart?" he asked Issa as she perused the menu.

"Got anything vegetarian?"

"Hmmm. I guess I could check with the herbalist to see if she's got any tofu," Mister P. said, the grimace plainly displayed so that anyone could tell that he thought this was a bad idea.

"I don't eat tofu."

"Well, we could use mushrooms as a substitute. It might be tasty if we battered and fried—"

"Mushrooms give me hives," she interrupted.

"Peppers and onions?" he asked.

"Gas."

"Well, girl, what do you eat?"

"Potatoes."

Theo looked at Issa and rolled his eyes, then pointed at her non-vegan totally made of cow skin leather shoes. She shrugged.

"They're thrifted!"

Chapter 9
Fizzy Lemons

Theo and Issa found the only empty table in the tiny stall and devoured their meal, delighted at the slight buoyancy the fizzy lemons gave them as they ate. Their knees kept knocking into the table as they floated just barely above their seats.

"So what do you think the reader is gonna say?" Issa asked Theo through her mouthful of fries.

He shrugged. "Does it matter?"

"It could go either way. They see, like, a million possibilities and then tell you which one they think your parents are most likely to not freak out about if they hear it or, better yet, the one that means you'll come back and pay for another reading."

"So you think they lie?" he asked.

"No. I just think that there's no way that they can ever be totally right. Okay, so, let's say the reader says I'm going to be hit by a car. So, Aunt Ionie drives me to school that day, or Mama keeps me home sick. Now, I don't get hit by a car. Was the reader right, or did she just choose one of the unlikeliest timelines to give? Aunt Cedella loves a good reading. She uses us as an excuse to go get love advice. I overheard Aunt Ionie say that she had to watch her to make sure she didn't spend all her money there."

Theo couldn't think of a dumber reason to go see a reader. "I don't believe you."

Issa stuffed a fry into her mouth. "Believe what you want."

Theo was about to argue with her a bit more when the entire stall fell to a hush as a man stumbled in, a barely crusted-over gash in his head. He crashed into the first table and sent a basket of fries flying into the air.

"Did you see her?" he growled at the couple who were sitting there. He moved to the next table.

"You saw her. You had to!" he shouted, but those people shook their heads too. Finally, he pointed his dirty, pudgy finger at Theo and wailed.

"Medium! Medium! You saw her. You saw the hag!"

The man was dirty, but not in the way that Theo and Issa had been earlier. This wasn't the filth of a dirty job or bad weather. This was the nastiness of weeks and weeks of neglect. He smelled like a cross between sour clothes left in the washer too long and raw meat left to rot at the bottom of a trash can. His eyes were bloodshot, and his nails were caked with muck. His hair looked like it had never been washed, but peculiarly his teeth were dove white, bleached like bones left to bake in the sun. He had his eyes trained on Theo, a fact that counteracted any effect of the fizzy lemon and sent him crashing into his seat with fear.

"You saw the hag, didn't you, boy?" he accused as he stalked ever closer, and then he began to sing. "Fair of hair she was so pretty, a princess not of air and berry, she stalked by day and stole by night, parents hold your children tight. Faiiiiir of haiiiirrrr—"

Mister P. placed his hand on the filthy man's shoulder. "That's enough, Marlen," he said softly. "That's enough. Why don't you come back here and get you something to eat?"

"But—but—the boy. He can see. I know he can. You saw her, didn't you, boy? You'll tell her you saw me. Give her a message?" he asked.

Mister P. stepped in between the man and Theo, using his body to block the filthy man's view.

"Now, now. Leave the boy alone. I don't think he can help you."

"But he can!" the man shouted and smashed his fist onto the food counter, causing the condiments to shake. "She stole my boy."

Mister P. dug his heels in then, pushing the man rather than guiding him, but the man didn't put up a fight. He just leaned over Mister P.'s shoulder so Theo could see him more clearly as he screamed.

"You tell her! I did! I searched. Faiiiiiiiiiir of haiiiiiirrrrr . . ." he sang, and his voice waned as Mister P. pulled him farther and farther out of sight.

"You okay?" Issa asked.

Theo nodded. It was easier to lie if he didn't have to speak.

"You don't think he's talking about our ghost?" Issa asked.

Theo shook his head, glad that his heart was starting to return to its normal rhythm.

"No. How would he know? I mean, there's no way he could know, could he?"

Theo and Issa cleaned off the table and made their way back onto the cobblestone path. It was almost one o'clock, and they didn't want to be late. Aunt Cedella might tack on an extra day of service, and there was no way they'd volunteer for that.

The reader was on the opposite side of the market, where the apprentice shops were. These were places where you learned how to become a better tarot reader or a better spell caster. You might come and get a hex removed or see one of the architects to help you build a house that repelled bad spirits and curses. Femi had a weekly appointment with one of the mind-reading schools, if you could call it that. It was more like a book club, given how few people ever received that particular gift.

The market was split into five sections. The food stalls were in one section, a mishmash of lopsided tents, food trucks, and vardo wagons bedecked in cowrie shells and painted in candy-colored adinkra symbols. Another section contained the hospital, which was not a single building but a collection of two-story longhouses with wrought iron balconies draped in kudzu. The beehive-shaped zoo enclosure made up another section, where magical pets were sold and exhibited. The fourth section contained the halls of sacred seers, churches and worship houses of different faiths that dated back to the earliest days of the market, along with gambling houses, bars, dance clubs, and matchmaking offices. The final section housed the scholars. Each building was designed by famed Haitian architect and telekinetic Georges Baussan in the gingerbread style with long porches and hanging latticework that looked like cake icing.

As happy as Theo and Issa had been while eating their lunch, they were equally despondent as they turned the corner onto Scholar Street. They passed the first house so intent on looking at their feet that they didn't notice the boy waving them down.

"Hey!"

Theo looked up and smiled.

"Hey, Romare," he said and dapped up his old classmate from Saturday school. From third to fifth grade, it was expected that all witches, warlocks, Bikin, and brujos spend each Saturday learning about the history of magical people and how to not only hone your gift but, more importantly, hide it. "You remember my cousin Issa."

"'Sup, Issa?"

Issa waved half-heartedly.

"You get a reading?" Theo asked, noticing that Romare had come out of Madame Moussad's, one of Aunt Ionie's favorite psychics.

Romare shook his head and pointed his finger at the sky. He twisted it around and around until a tiny tornado appeared on the tip of his finger and then petered out.

"My powers are on the fritz. I can do small tornadoes or start a small rainstorm, but nothing major. My mama thinks I'm sick."

Theo's eyebrows rose. Kids like them almost never got sick.

"What'd Madame say?" Theo asked.

Romare shrugged. "She said there's some shift in the temporal energies, and now that Mars is in retrograde, I should try to meditate more. Then she gave me a prescription I'm supposed to fill at the apothecary."

A wild peacock strutted down the middle of the street and squealed at them. Romare puffed out his cheeks and blew a massive gale that sent the land-bound bird up a few feet. It flapped its tiny blue-green wings in terror just as Romare's mom came tearing out of Madame's front door.

"Stop that! Probably why you're sick now. Torturing defenseless creatures."

"Bruuuuuh," Romare whined, and Theo had to stifle a laugh.

"Bruh? Who's a bruh? I'm your mother. I don't know what's gotten into you this week. Bruh?"

"Hey, Ms. Carlisle."

"Good afternoon, Theo, Issa. I haven't seen you in a while. You should come and visit us. I don't believe we've ever had you and your aunts over for Sunday dinner."

Theo squinted and wondered where he'd seen her lately. It was the park with Billy and the couple. She looked different that day, but it was definitely her.

"No ma'am," he said.

"That's settled then. I'll call your aunt—well, one of them, and work out the details. Romare spends too much time with kids who aren't like us. Playing Xbox and whatnot."

"Whatnot is fun," Romare replied. He smiled, and despite herself, Ms. Carlisle smiled back.

Romare waved good-bye as his mother dragged him off just in time for Issa to get picked up off her feet by a man.

Chapter 10
A Crow's Call

"Uncle Mack, put me down!" Issa screeched.

Uncle Mack, Aunt Cedella's second husband, laughed so loud his voice rattled the pebbles in the concrete. A huge man with an even bigger grin, Uncle Mack set Issa down on her feet gently and faked a jab at Theo, which Theo easily swatted away.

"What you two doin' down here today?" he asked.

"Getting a reading," Issa said as she tried to smooth her hair back into place.

Uncle Mack looked around them and down the street like he was looking for someone. "Honey brought you here, or Ionie?" he asked. Honey was Uncle Mack's nickname for Aunt Cedella on account of the color of her eyes. Theo could never really tell if his aunt loved the name or hated it.

"Aunt Cedella," Theo replied, knowing that Uncle Mack was still trying to get into his aunt's good graces and would probably be sniffing around them both all day until he got a chance to talk to her.

"Y'all must a done something real stupid if you down here. Yup, can't be nothing *but* a reading, looking at those hangdog faces."

Theo and Issa nodded.

"We're supposed to see Granddaddy after," Issa said.

"Mr. Ruben? Oh, I know I got to hang with you then. Let's go see him first."

Theo shook his head. It was twelve forty-five already. "Our appointment is at one, and we can't miss it or we'll have to do service with Queen Chet again next week."

Uncle Mack laughed again, rattling the branches on Tituba's oak at the end of the street. Ghostly and majestic, the Spanish moss on the tree shivered at Uncle Mack's sonic vibrations, almost like it was yawning. The tree was said to be over five hundred years old, even older than the angel oak on John's Island, and was as wide as a dump truck all around.

"Y'all must have gotten into all the fun to get that kinda punishment. I tell you what. Let's go in early and see if she can fit you in, then I'll walk you down to Mr. Ruben's."

Theo and Issa walked with Uncle Mack to the end of the street, where Mr. Charlie's office was located inside the oldest house on the block, Mother Mourning's Tea House. Unlike the haint blue and salamander colors of the houses next to them, the tea house was black with white adinkra symbols painted on every beam and board. Black lace curtains fluttered out of the sitting room windows and made it look as if the house was throbbing like a heartbeat. Theo took a step onto the porch and shivered.

Mr. Charlie told fortunes out of the second floor apartment in Mother Mourning's Tea House, and while most psychics had a check-in system with a host or secretary who checked your name off—some of the younger ones even had a number you'd text—Mr. Charlie used a monkey.

"What's with the monkey?" Uncle Mack asked, and Issa dropped her head in irritation. She hated the monkey.

"You have to tell it your name, and then it runs back into the room through that little door."

"Noooo," Uncle Mack said in disbelief. "I don't believe you."

Theo walked up to the little monkey in the high-chair in front of the door. He was wearing a tiny denim jumpsuit and a plum-sized cap. He was munching excitedly on popcorn from a plastic bag and didn't pay the three of them any attention until Theo got almost nose to nose with him.

"We have a one o'clock appointment with Mr. Charlie. Theo Tatterly and Issa Igwe."

The monkey munched loudly on his handful of popcorn and squinted at Theo with his watery eyes before he hopped down from the chair and disappeared through a tiny door set inside the larger office door.

"I don't believe it," Uncle Mack said. "I don't know if it's cute, crazy, or something else."

"It's definitely something else," Issa commented.

A moment later the door opened.

Theo, Issa, and Uncle Mack walked into the parlor, which was just a large room with a round table in the middle. There was a tattered couch with seats so old they'd fallen in the middle, like someone had taken an ice cream scooper and dug out the stuffing in each one. A large black chandelier, tinkling with glass shards and black freshwater pearls, hung majestically above the table as a countermeasure in elegance. It looked like it was left there to show you what Mother Mourning had intended the room to look like if it weren't for Mr. Charlie taking over the space.

Like in most reading rooms, various tools of the trade were sitting on the shelves attached to the wall: crystal balls of all sizes; tarot cards; astrological charts, some in books, some in scrolls; tins filled with teas from all over the world, along with various mugs, cups, and kettles; wax for ceromancy; and finally a large floor-to-ceiling cage of doves.

Uncle Max nudged Theo and pointed. "You don't see that every day. I haven't had a reading by a true augur in years. Now that's a rare talent."

"How does it work?" Issa asked.

"Supposedly they have some kind of connection with the birds, and once they release them, the flight pattern can give you signs. Old magic."

"I prefer hydromancy. It's cleaner," she said, referring to fortune-telling by water. The seeker drops a pebble into a body of water, and the psychic reads the ripples.

Theo snorted. "You just like skipping stones."

Issa opened her mouth to say something, her mouth curled in what could have been an amazing comeback, but Mr. Charlie chose that moment to step into the room and sneeze heartily into his handkerchief.

"Bless you," they all said.

He was as tall as Uncle Mack but reedy, with thin arms, sticklike legs, and a shiny bald head. The overalls he had on were two sizes too big, and he seemed to swim in them as he walked. He stuffed the handkerchief in the chest pocket as he sat down in the largest chair at the round table.

"Oh, well. I didn't expect all of you today."

"We had an appointment. My aunt Cedella sent us," Theo said.

Mr. Charlie nodded. "Yes, yes. Mr. Furry Bottom told me."

Issa slapped her hand over her mouth so a giggle wouldn't escape, and Uncle Mack just smiled.

"I meant I just wasn't expecting you both at once. And who is your chaperone?"

"I'm their uncle," Uncle Mack replied.

"Hmmm. I didn't think the Tatterly family had any older boys in the States. Ah, a paramour. Who did you . . . Oh, no, I've got it. Cedella. Keep at it. I see possibilities. Given that thing in November turns out well enough. Yes, yes, possibilities. Okay. Which one of you is first?"

Issa raised her hand.

"Well, come on up. Cedella likes a full report, so I'll be dictating as well."

He snapped his fingers, and a twin image of him appeared in the seat next to him, only the image was a little watery so you could see through it.

Uncle Mack whistled. "Impressive," he whispered.

The darker image of Mr. Charlie picked up a notepad and sat at the ready while watery Mr. Charlie beckoned Issa over so that she sat opposite him. He took a deep breath.

"I want you to close your eyes and clear your mind, dear. Set your hands on the table, palms up, and when I say a word, you say the first word that comes to mind. If it's a name, say that as well. Understand?"

"Yes sir," Issa replied before closing her eyes.

They were both silent for so long Theo began to nod off to sleep, but Mr. Charlie spoke up soon enough.

"Red," he said.

"Robin," Issa replied.

"Carrot," he said.

"Cake," she replied.

They went on like that for a few rounds before Mr. Charlie threw out a word that made Issa think.

"Ghost."

The corners of Issa's mouth twitched, and she shook her head as if she were saying no. Then she stood up, though she kept her eyes closed, and then she sat down. Her head dropped as if she'd fallen asleep, and when she raised it to speak, someone else's voice came out.

"Ela vem para roubar. Ela vem para matar. Ela vem para destruir."

Theo and Uncle Mack stood up. They'd both seen Issa overtaken by a spirit, but this felt different. This spirit was restless and scared. That was dangerous.

Mr. Charlie didn't flinch. He just kept writing in his pad in one body and kept his eyes closed in the other.

"What is your name?" he asked.

Issa opened her mouth and coughed. A cloud of black smoke erupted from her throat and circled above the table like a thundercloud.

"She comes," Issa said in a strange accent. She looked around the room but seemed to not see them.

"What is your name?" Mr. Charlie asked again, but this time Issa screamed, her voice rising so loud that Theo had to cover his ears. The swirling black cloud cracked and formed into a dozen black crows that flew out the window. Mr. Charlie jumped from his seat to watch them fly away, and then whispered into his twin's ear. He walked into the other room and returned with a kettle and two cups.

He sat one cup in front of Issa, whose eyes were unfocused and unblinking. He poured her a cup and then himself a cup before he sat down.

"Issa, I know you're in there. You should be able to smell the lemon balm in that teacup. I would like you to come and sit with me. Please come and sit with me."

"She comes," Issa said again in that strange voice.

"Yes, I heard. Thank you, dear, but it's time for Issa to come back. I would like very much to speak with her instead. I've received your message. You may leave now."

Issa's eyebrows scrunched in confusion, and then she sniffed and twitched her nose at the rising steam in the cup. A second later she slumped down in her chair, her chin resting on her chest.

"Yes, that's it, Issa. Come and take a sip of that tea. Breathe in that lemony goodness."

With eyes still closed, Issa grasped the cup, and then slowly opened her eyes.

Mr. Charlie smiled, then turned to Theo.

"All right. Your turn."

Chapter 11
Kiyoberu

Uncle Mack looked at Theo and raised his eyebrows. It was a silent question. Maybe *Are you ready for this?* Or it could have been *This dude's crazy pants. You wanna rush him?*

Theo wasn't used to shying away from a challenge, so he shrugged and walked toward the table, just as Issa stood up, teacup in hand. She seemed to shiver a little as she took a sip.

"You okay?" he asked.

She nodded, though she looked a little unsteady on her feet.

"C'mon, Little Bit. I'll get you some boiled peanuts from the stall on the corner. It'll be good to get you some fresh air," Uncle Mack said as he took Issa under his arm.

He turned to the psychic. "Mr. Charlie, was that, uh . . . normal?" he asked.

Mr. Charlie was whispering with himself in the other chair and held up his finger as he finished whatever he had to say.

"Oh, yes. She'll be fine. As you've said, a little snack can't hurt. Ta!" Mr. Charlie said brightly.

Uncle Mack grumbled. "Yeah. Ta."

Theo scooted his seat closer to the table and swallowed hard. Mr. Charlie smiled warmly, and Theo noticed two gold teeth winking from the back of his mouth. He couldn't really say why, but it calmed him.

"So, Mr. Tatterly. No need to be nervous."

"I'm not nervous."

"No need to lie to me either. I'm psychic, remember."

"Yes sir."

"Now, my process will be quite different for you than it was for your cousin. Every person is different, and readings for Bikin like you and Issa require a practiced hand. Have you had your tea leaves read before?"

Theo shook his head.

"Perfect. Let me get another cup."

Mr. Charlie left for a moment and came back with a cheerful yellow cup with a chipped rim and cherries painted on the side. He poured the tea into Theo's cup and bade him to drink. It tasted like blueberries but smelled like honeysuckle.

"Is this the same tea you gave Issa?" Theo asked.

Mr. Charlie shook his head. "Don't worry about that. Tell me about this hag you've seen."

Theo coughed, the tea scalding his windpipe.

"I— How did you . . . ?"

Mr. Charlie tapped the side of his head.

"Psychic!" he sang.

"Umm . . . She was a ghost, but not like the other ghosts I see. She could, um, move things. And she looked like she was rotting. Ghosts can't rot. They don't have bodies. I think."

"Quite right. Most ghosts lack a corporeal form, but there is a spirit with a particularly vicious nature that can feed on negative energy and over time become solid."

Theo sipped his tea and felt his head swim. For a moment he was in a chair, having a talk with Mr. Charlie, and the next moment he and Mr. Charlie were hovering above the table together in a swirl of blue light. He thought to mention it, but the urge passed quickly.

"I never read about any solid spirits."

Mr. Charlie nodded. "They are quite rare, but they've existed as far back as Moses parting the Red Sea."

The blue light then filled the room and turned black just before exploding into a riot of stars. Mr. Charlie pointed to a constellation just as a comet shot across the sky. "This is God's Back. Some call it the Milky Way; others say one of the first people walked out of heaven and pressed her footprints into the sky, and if you're born under the right star, you can unlock the path that will lead you there. Why is this important? Because you were born under the right star, and that is why you will also be chased by wayward ghosts and spirits, some benign and some unimaginably evil."

Theo, whose head had started to spin, considered Mr. Charlie's statement. "Or they're just balls of gas," he said.

"Perhaps," Mr. Charlie replied. "But let's assume I'm right and you're too young to know anything. Your star chart was especially fun to decipher. I had to use my Borana calendar to get everything just right. It comes from the Borana Ormo people of Ethiopia and Northern Kenya. There are no weeks in the calendar. Delicious fun, but tedious since there is a different name for each day in the month, and those are all in Turkana. Have you ever been to Kenya? I haven't, and summoning Kenyan ghosts to aid in translation is its own kind of tedium. But to the business at hand. Your father has passed on to the ancestral realm, but how much do you know of him?"

Theo shrugged. He didn't like to talk about his father.

Mr. Charlie nodded.

"Star charts are one thing, but family lines are another."

He drew a glowing line in the air with his finger, connecting stars to each other in a giant weblike tree. "There is a whole field of study for ancestral emotional alignment. Very interesting stuff. Your DNA holds the hurts and the triumphs of all the people whose DNA coalesced to make you. To correct a misalignment, the practitioner must call the names of those gone before."

Suddenly the stars Mr. Charlie had connected morphed into glowing outlines of faces. Theo recognized his own.

"This is no easy feat for Black people on this continent whose names were changed or stolen, not to mention the impact of those not directly in the DNA but no less impactful on the expression of that genetic code through caretaking and adoption. Very interesting stuff."

Theo was getting lost. "What does this have to do with the ghost or my dad?"

"Well, not necessarily your father, but all your fathers and uncles. You are the last male Tatterly in the line. That is no insignificant place to be. I believe it may have made you vulnerable to more than one supernatural entity. I've consulted with one or two of my colleagues in the market, and they've sensed this presence before among your family, but never this strong. Something malevolent is drawn to your family and maybe directing evil intent your way.

"Your ghost is called a kiyoberu, a crying woman. Her grief over some great injustice or harm keeps her from passing on, and she feeds on the grief of others to gain enough power to rise from the dead."

"Great. She has a name. If she's got a name, then she can be exorcised." Theo was excited. He began to think of three older exorcists he had taken summer workshops with that were probably not too far away. His thumbs itched to text them.

Mr. Charlie took the last sip of his tea and let the cup drop into oblivion below him as he shook his head.

"Stay far away from her."

"But why?" Theo all but croaked.

"The ghost is one thing, but she is being controlled by something far more powerful, and for that, I have no name. I am afraid you're at a crossroads. From what I can see you will either open a door to great magical success, or this could be the end of the Tatterly line forever. Kiyoberus are very powerful. They deal with demigods and demons. They work in thin places on lay lines that haven't even been charted. If you face her, there is only a fifty-fifty chance of success. My advice is to avoid it."

"But your face doesn't agree. What are my chances if I avoid her?"

"Fifty-fifty."

"Fifty-fifty what?"

"Life or death."

"And my family?

Mr. Charlie took a sip of his tea and gave a short shake of his head.

"This is why I must make a modified report to your aunt. If I tell her the truth, she will interfere in your decision and make the situation more dire than it already is. You must make this decision alone. Because it is you who will suffer the consequences."

Mr. Charlie snapped his fingers, and they both fell out of orbit, plummeting to the earth below at a speed so terrifyingly fierce that Theo's eyes began to water. He couldn't even scream, because it was impossible to draw in a breath of air. Before he had a chance to give in to the panic, he bounced lightly in his chair at the round table, as if he'd only stood and sat down again.

"W-wa—"

Mr. Charlie leaned back in his chair and whispered to his twin self, who had been diligently recording the entire session. The other Mr. Charlie nodded and then ripped out the sheet of paper he'd been scribbling on and crumpled it. He stood up, sat atop his twin, and disappeared.

"This is important, and this message is only for you and not your aunts or anyone else. My gossip spirits are whispering. I don't like what I'm hearing out there. You are dealing with a kiyoberu, a child thief. Kiyoberus are attachment spirits. They can sometimes cling to the living. She will come for you and for the people around you, especially Issa. Your cousin is a special kind of conduit. She's her chance for a solid, living, breathing body, so you must be careful. Through her, this spirit could tear down cities."

Theo looked into the man's watery eyes to see if he could sense a lie there or a hint of insanity that might let him off the hook. If he could tease out a bit of doubt, he could forget about this death mission. Who chooses a death mission? Nobody. Mr. Charlie's lip quirked, probably listening in to every word Theo was thinking. Mr. Charlie got up from the table, walked over to his bookshelf, and pulled down a slim green leather book with akoben, the war horn adinkra symbol, burned into the front. It symbolized wariness and vigilance. He licked his finger, turned to a page, and snapped a picture.

"I'll send this to your phone. Memorize it. It's everything you need to know about kiyoberus."

excerpted from the *Book of Hags, Banshees, and Malevolent Rooted Spirits*

Description:

A terenne class demon most often originating in the brief periods before the end of a war and the few years after. It prefers ruins, construction sites, and otherwise demolished areas. It can be tied to sources of water, but it does not have to be. It can take several forms, sometimes their original physical selves and at other times the form of a small pig or boar.

As a revenge demon it must be fed a fresh crop of souls until it reaches a specific number tied to its curse origin. The curse will most often be the result of a failed bargain with a higher demon or low-level god or goddess.

Is drawn to: sea life, crowds, burial sites, ancient or older ruins, movement, fermentation (beer, rising bread, pickling spices, kimchi), and sea salt

Repelled by: terrestrial life (warm-blooded animals, especially felines), desert salt, fresh flowers, rope, other spirit creatures, and magical wildlife

Mr. Charlie took out a notepad and scribbled down some notes, then handed it to Theo.

"I assume you know what a gris-gris bag is? For protection?"

Theo scrunched up his nose. He knew of them but had never made one himself. Aunt Ionie carried one all day, every day, but he hadn't asked her how to make one of his own.

Mr. Charlie rolled his eyes and pointed to each line.

"You'll need a carrying case. Traditionally it's a bag you hang around your neck so the bag can hang near your heart, but that's not necessary. You'll need a base of either salt or fragrant wood. Salt is good for sweeter spirits, and wood for hard hearts. You'll need the blood of an ancestor. Now I don't mean real blood, but something with their DNA: hair, tears, a fingernail will do. And other sentimental items. It will come to you as you mix.

"Now!" he said and clapped his hands before taking a breath. "Here is the faux prophecy your aunt so desperately wants for you. You'll repeat it exactly as I tell you even though not a word of it is true. It is what she needs to hear, but not what she wants to hear."

"That doesn't make any sense."

"It's not supposed to."

Chapter 12
Small Gods

Theo walked out of Mother Mourning's Tea House confused and not at all ready for Aunt Cedella's questions.

She stood there in the weird pinkish-blue afternoon light of the market, tapping her foot on the cobblestones.

"I told you two to stay together, didn't I?" she asked. It wasn't a question he was meant to answer, so Theo kept his mouth shut and followed her toward Tituba's oak.

"I already talked to Uncle Mack. He bought Issa some boiled peanuts and went to visit with Granddad. Lord knows Daddy loves that man. I do not know why."

Probably because *she* loved that man, Theo thought, but there was no way anyone could bribe him to say it out loud.

Granddad lived near the market but not in it. As one of the first families, the Tatterlys had claim to some of the land on the island, and a few members of his family and others lived there and never left. They thought the island was safer, and sometimes when America was raging and the South was showing its ugliest face, it was hard to argue that it wasn't, but Theo thought living this far from other people had to be isolating.

Ambrose Remington Tatterly lived in a two-bedroom flamingo-pink shotgun house covered in honeysuckle and wild purple maypops. A warding spell kept the mosquitoes away, but it did nothing for the frogs, lizards, and ladybugs which swarmed so bad that sometimes they blackened the windows. His wife, Nana Mae, also kept bees somewhere on the property, so there was always the low hum of flapping wings in the background. Theo made a note to himself to ask her for some of her homemade candle wax. Sadhya Auntie would want some for the care packages she sent to her legion of cousins scattered across the globe in boarding schools.

The place was surrounded by a low wrought iron fence that no one, not even family, could cross, so Aunt Cedella just yelled.

"Daddy! Open the gate. Daddy!"

"Hold on, hold on. I was just chattin' with my grand-baby on the back porch."

"You know this extra security isn't necessary, Daddy. The market will keep everybody who means you harm away."

Ambrose Tatterly harrumphed, his bald head shining in the dimming light. "Look at you. Tellin' me, a grown person, what he needs and don't need."

"I been grown some time now, Daddy."

"Says you. From my side, it looks like you got a lot to learn. You don't never leave your security up to some-body else," he said as he rounded the corner to make his way to the front gate. He pointed his cane at Theo.

"You'll do well to remember that. You never, ever leave something that's important up to someone else. You take care of it yourself so you know exactly what to expect. Got it?" he asked.

"Got it, Granddad," Theo replied.

Aunt Cedella threw her hands in the air as she stomped through the now open gate. "Fine, Daddy, king of all security."

"Watch that tone, girl. You ain't too big to beat."

Aunt Cedella stopped and dropped a kiss on the old man's grizzly cheek and then wiped off the lipstick with her thumb.

"You know I just worry about you."

"Worry 'bout yourself," he grumbled, then he leaned down to pull Theo into a rough half-hug. "How ya doin', Bright Eye?"

"Fine," Theo said into his grandfather's armpit. Bright Eye was Theo's other nickname. A posse of beetles flew into the air in a glittering blue cloud. One landed on Theo's arm, and he raised his hand to swat it. Granddad snatched his wrist just in time.

"Don't you dare, boy. Don't you know beetles are sacred? If you ever in battle, you want them around. They symbolize rebirth and regeneration."

"It's a bug."

"A god don't have to be big to be powerful," he said and softly sent the beetle on its way with a finger. "Issa's 'round back. I put some shrimps on. Got a bit a sausage for ya. Put some hair on that chest. How old are you now? Seventeen? Twenty-five?" he asked.

Theo shook his head. "Twelve."

"That old, huh? I guess I better tell you the Tatterly men's secret to life then."

Granddad took hold of Theo's shoulders and looked him in the eye, and they both said together, "Protect your nuts."

They both laughed hard at their old joke and then walked to the backyard, Theo slowing his pace to match his grandfather's.

"How'd that reading go? Issa came back all shook up. I told Cedella that mess ain't worth a d—uh, darn."

"Fine. Ran into Romare and his mom, then Uncle Mack found us." Theo closed the space between him and his granddad so he couldn't be overheard. "You don't believe the psychics at all?" Theo asked, remembering what Issa had said earlier.

"I ever tell you about my uncle Bertram?"

Theo shook his head.

"Uncle Bertram was my nana's brother on Granny Ellison's side. He died long before you was even thought of. Thing is, he had a reading when he turned eighteen that said he was gone drown on his birthday. So, young boy that he was, he lived it up that whole year. Drove his mama insane with his antics, drinkin' and carryin' on with all kinda girls 'round town. Gave up a scholarship to Benedict College. Had no less than two upset fathers banging on Granny's door on behalf of their daughters. But then his nineteenth birthday came and his heart kept beating. Twentieth, twenty-fifth, thirtieth birthday, and he was still breathing. Hit a rough patch and decided to take a cruise on his fortieth. Temptin' God, as they say, and nothing doin', he was still there, but that old woman's words were still in the back of his head, so he didn't marry, never had any children. Gave up swimmin' and fishing, and then he got so old that it seemed like maybe she was wrong. He lived to be ninety-five."

"Well, how did he die?"

"Slipped and fell in the tub. Point is, he could have had a life, a home, no criminal record. He could a gone to college, had some battles, had some real loves if it wasn't for that reading. She was right. Dead on, but he'da been better off if he never knew."

"So, I can just ignore it—what the seer told me?" Theo asked, slightly hopeful.

Granddad shrugged a bit and then sucked his teeth real loud like something had gotten stuck up there. "I dunno about that. Once you know something it's real hard to unknow it. Got something you want to tell me, son?" he asked.

"Uh—"

Theo was about to tell him what Mr. Charlie said when the breeze picked up, smelling of wild onions and something rotten. Granddad sniffed the air and looked into the trees, searching. Then he tapped his cane against the fence, sending a rattle along every bar that rang in time with the windchimes hanging from the porch and the whistle of the bottle tree at the edge of the yard.

Nana Mae stepped out onto the back deck with a tray of thumbprint cookies and whistled. The rattling and the wind came to a stop and she smiled.

"Wild spirits out there today. I guess my baby, Theo, must be here."

Theo smiled back and grabbed two cookies from the tray before Issa could eat them all. Nana Mae was Granddad's second wife, and she and the aunts didn't always get along. But she was the only living grandmother Theo had, and she played her part just fine, if you asked him.

"I'm so glad you're finally here. I got something for you and Issa," she told him.

"Those award-winning jam cookies are more than a little something. I might have to drop on by more often," Uncle Mack teased. Aunt Cedella rolled her eyes.

"Mae, these really are the best cookies you've ever made. I would love the recipe. I got a potluck coming up at work, and I need something good. I've been looking for a base for my bravery cookie. One of the kindergarten teachers in town asked me for something to help her new students when they show up mid-year."

"Sure thing. I'm bakery royalty, and this recipe is guaranteed to win stomachs, if not hearts."

"You said you had something for us, Nana Mae," Issa interrupted.

Theo looked over at his cousin to make sure she really was all right from earlier. She put on a good show, but Theo could see the whites of her eyes weren't the same, and there was a tremor in her voice. She was faking.

"You good?" he asked. He moved closer to her while Nana Mae ran back in the house and came back out with two cardboard boxes with holes cut in the top.

"I'm fine," she whispered. She nudged him with her elbow to get some space between them. Aunt Cedella, despite herself, was laughing with Uncle Mack at the little iron table in the backyard while Granddad tried lighting the grill with a whisper.

Nana Mae presented a long rectangular box to Theo and a box the size of a loaf of bread to Issa.

"Don't just stand there. Open 'em. This is from me and Granddad."

Theo ripped the lid of his box off, and that's when the snake jumped out.

Chapter 13

Protectors

Theo jumped back, and Nana Mae suspended the snake in the air, freezing him in mid-jump.

Granddad laughed so hard he fell into a coughing fit. Aunt Cedella had to run into the house to get him a glass of lemonade.

"I can't believe you're scared of such a lil' bitty old snake," Nana Mae scolded.

"But, Nana Mae. It's a snake. Snakes *are* scary."

"He is not scary. His name is Rupert. He's your new pet."

"I don't need a bloodsucking pet," Theo retorted.

"Oh, stop being dramatic. He's just a little old corn snake. Look at that color. Isn't he beautiful?" She beamed.

Theo could admit the snake was pretty with its orange and reddish markings, but that didn't mean he was going to snuggle with the thing.

"You sure he doesn't bite?"

"Well, of course, he bites—he's a snake. But corn snakes are great pets. He won't attack you or anything, and he doesn't get that big, so you can keep him in a pocket if you want to take him to school or out and about."

"Do people do that?" Theo asked.

She nodded. "People like you do, or at least they should. Young people forget about the old ways once they get access to the internet and cell phones and Book-Face and whatever. A snake is the best friend a medium can ever have. You exist at the doorway between two worlds, the living and the dead, and so does he. You keep him close, and he will give you strength."

Theo opened his mouth to say *no thank you* but closed it as he caught a reproachful look from Aunt Cedella. He pressed his lips together hard so he wouldn't be tempted to say anything, and just smiled awkwardly as he plucked the snake out of the air and held him in both hands.

"If there is a snake in this box, Nana Mae, I'm gonna pass out," Issa said loudly.

Nana Mae chuckled. "Nope. Not for you. Check it out."

Issa opened her box and a smile fit to rival the sun broke out on her face. It was a tiny orange honey-eyed kitten.

"Oh, Nana Mae, I love her!" she squealed.

"I knew you would. She also lives between two worlds. But this one is a protector. Keep her close. She'll keep you from being preyed upon by unwanted ghosts. Now, kittens aren't as easy to wrangle as snakes, so come on inside for a minute and I'll tell you how to keep her close, and you can tell me what's got you upset."

"I'm not upset. Why does everybody keep saying that?"

"Mm-hmm. Just come on in here."

Theo caught Aunt Cedella looking up at Uncle Mack with a softness that she reserved just for him. When she noticed Theo looking, she backed up and turned to the grill.

"Come on over here and get something to eat," she called out to Theo, like she hadn't just been caught.

Uncle Mack sat on Granddad's joggling board and whistled. A plate caught the wind and landed on the bench in front of him as he rocked on the unsteady board.

"I didn't know you were telekinetic," Theo said, a little impressed.

Uncle Mack laughed. "I'm not, not really. Magic is all around us. I can teach you how to use the currents in the air to move things. It's simple. Real easy."

Aunt Cedella sucked her teeth. "It may be simple, but it ain't easy."

"I'll show you, Boy. She just mad she can't do it. Might need it to keep them real estate poachers away."

Granddad's ears perked up. "They been sniffin' around again. Cedella, you ain't tell me anything was goin' on."

Aunt Cedella looked like she was caught sneaking in late after curfew. Granddad was the only person Theo had seen make her nervous.

"Nothin' more than usual, Daddy. Just an inquiry from the city. That's all. I put a charm up, and Ionie's already looking for the deed."

"That house already has a charm on it stronger than concrete-covered steel."

Theo looked at Granddad as the old man read the uncertainty on his oldest child's face, and Theo's stomach sank. It was the first time he'd ever seen the man look like he didn't have all the answers.

"Well, Baby Girl. About that," he said as he waved Cedella over to him and out of earshot. Whatever he had to say, it wasn't good, and by the furrow digging into Aunt Cedella's forehead, he knew that this was serious business they'd never willingly discuss with him.

By the time Theo got home, Aunt Ionie had already purchased a terrarium for Rupert with a little warming light and water bowl shaped like a stone. Great-Aunt Trudy Anne was so excited she spent an hour sticking her hand in and out of the cage just so Rupert could stick out his tongue at her.

"Nana Mae says I should take him with me when I leave the house."

Great-Aunt Trudy Anne nodded enthusiastically.

"He'll make you strong," she said and then put her arms up to flex her biceps, though you couldn't really see any biceps because of her shawl and all.

There was a knock on the door, even though it was cracked open. It was Aunt Sabrina. Her head was wrapped up in an emerald and yellow ankara scarf, and her fingernails were crusted with dried paint. She almost always kept her hair covered in a scarf. Granddad's father had gifted her his pocket watch, and it hung around her neck. She was so sensitive to premonitions it helped her to keep hold of where and when she was at all times. Theo could tell she hadn't been sleeping. There were dark bags under her eyes.

"Heard about your adventures. Glad you got to see Romare again too. Been a while since you guys had conjure lessons together. Last time I talked to his mom, she said she might be thinking of transferring him to Robert Smalls."

"Really? Why?"

"I guess her swanky private school in West Ashley ain't all it's cracked up to be. Not too many of *us* there, if you know what I mean. How was Queen Chet?" Her voice was hoarse, like she hadn't used it in a while. A premonition was riding her.

"Uh . . ." Theo thought about it. He wanted to say *crazy*, but Aunt Sabrina had taught him that the word was insensitive to people who had mental illnesses. "Rowdy and reckless."

Aunt Sabrina chuckled. "Good words. She is that. I don't know about reckless, though. She seems to always have a plan."

"I guess."

"Got a new pet, I see. What's her name?"

"His name's Rupert. Nana Mae gave him to me. Great-Aunt Trudy Anne says he's supposed to make me strong."

"He's a protector." She tapped the glass and made a kissing noise at Rupert, who, for his part, perked up a bit and blinked his black eyes at her. "He can help amplify your efforts to send wayward souls on to the beyond and help keep you rooted right here in the land of the living."

"I got a reading today," he said.

Aunt Sabrina cut her eyes at him and held up her hand. "Don't tell me. You know you're not supposed to share the specifics. Your reading is for you."

"Granddad says I shouldn't pay attention to it."

"He tell you that story about Uncle Bertram?"

Theo nodded.

Aunt Sabrina rolled her eyes and sat next to him on the bed. "Uncle Bertram was a fool way before he ever got that reading and way after. The reading is for the person it's given to, and some of the interpretation can't just be left to the seer, you have to do some of the work too. What does your gut tell you? When you go to bed tonight and say your prayers, what is God whispering to you? Listen hard, and whatever you come up with is what you should do."

"What if I'm wrong?" Theo asked.

"You're a Tatterly, and Great-Aunt Trudy Anne has been talking to the dead since long before you were ever born. If you ever need any help, your name is all the currency you need to get the dead to help. Okay?"

"Okay."

"Feel any better?"

Theo scrunched up his face, and Aunt Sabrina rained down a flurry of tickles so fierce he almost peed himself.

The next morning Theo woke up to something scratching on his window. No, not scratching. He peeled his eyes open and adjusted to the sound. Tapping, maybe? He rolled out of bed and pushed the window open. It was Romare, arm cocked back to toss another handful of pebbles from the garden up at him.

"Hey! Come down. I got your text. Let's go play some ball."

Text?

Theo yawned, and Romare must have taken that as a yes, because he walked to the front of the house and out of sight.

Okay? Theo thought as he got dressed. A few minutes later he was yawning on the front porch in a pair of basketball shorts, face washed, after planting a kiss on Aunt Cedella's cheek as she read the paper.

"Ready?" Romare asked as he started walking. Theo followed, trying to shake the weirdness from his bones. Romare had never come over by himself before, and they'd never played ball before, but here he was. He wanted to ask if this was some trick or something, but that would be weirder than accepting the invitation, wouldn't it? He read a text from Issa and replied as they walked in silence to the park.

Romare show up?

Yeah, weird.

He's not weird. You're weird. I texted him from your phone at Granddad's. You're welcome.

But we're not ball friends.

Do you have ball friends?

Theo paused and thought about it before texting back. Issa had some nerve. She didn't have any friends either. They were both misfits. Theo just accepted it. Issa, on the other hand, was always trying to meet somebody until it blew up in her face. Theo knew better.

One—maybe

Now you got two. Don't be weird. Friends are good. And talk. People talk.

I don't really know him like that.

Get to know him then.

It was early, so there was still a court they could have all to themselves for a while, although the serious ballers and high school phenoms shooting for D1 college scholarships had been out since the sun came up. Through the wire fencing, Theo could see Billy swinging, just like he'd done for years, and that feeling at the back of his neck irked him, but he ignored it.

Theo tossed the ball straight at Romare's chest.

"Check!"

Romare caught it, and it was on.

"Who's your favorite Marvel character?" Theo asked as he shuffled in his defense squat, fingers loose.

Romare faked right, dribbled, and shot. "Doctor Strange, duh!" he yelled.

The ball bounced off the rim, and Theo caught it, sprinting for the other hoop. He shot for the three, feeling confident.

"Miss!" Romare grabbed the ball and walked it down the court. "You?"

"Scarlet Witch," Theo spat as he caught Romare in a fake and snatched the ball, dribbling fast to try to get a rhythm.

"Lame."

They both ran for the hoop. Theo jumped for the two, but Romare slapped the ball down.

"You just saying that 'cause she's a girl."

Romare laughed and bounced the ball between his legs. A little flashy for one-on-one.

"My mom's the most powerful person I know. It's not 'cause she's a girl. It's 'cause she doesn't use her power. What's the point of having it if you don't use it?"

Romare sprinted for the hoop, jumped, and with more hang time than is humanly possible without a little magic, dunked.

"Ay, that's not fair," Theo said, but his voice gave away how much he was impressed.

"Why not? I'm Bikin, you're Bikin."

"Somebody might see."

"They'll just think I'm the next LeBron."

Theo hung his head back in silence for a beat, and then they both burst out laughing.

"Aight, maybe not," Romare finally admitted. He tossed the ball to Theo. "What about DC?"

"Trash. The only character worth anything is Batman, and he's a psychopath."

"Truth."

"All that money and he builds a flying submarine. I mean, build a community center, my guy? Buy all the kids in the narrows bikes so they can outrun the gangsters. How much could it really cost?"

Romare laughed as he tried and failed to steal the ball. "Pay a PI to find out why Gotham got so many toxic waste spills."

They took a break and sat to catch their breaths.

"You go to the reader a lot?" Theo asked.

Romare shrugged. "What's a lot? Maybe once every few months."

"That's more than me. They say the same thing? You believe it?"

Romare scrunched up his forehead. "I know you're not supposed to tell anyone about your readings, but the last one used tarot cards, and I got the six of cups. It's supposed to mean friendship or whatever, and then I ran into you at the market and you texted. I mean, like, that's a big coincidence."

Theo didn't mention that it was Issa who texted, but maybe that was how the readings worked, by you working them. Just then Frank showed up with a couple of guys from school, and Theo got the rare pleasure of introducing someone to people he knew.

They played. They talked. Theo's favorite candy was Skittles. Romare liked Swedish Fish, which Theo roasted him about. No one liked Swedish Fish. Two kids from the public school joined in for two on two. They won, but Theo didn't care. They walked over to the pizza spot and ate lunch, then played some more, and by the time Theo looked up again it was nearly dinnertime. He didn't think about dead boys waiting to pass on, or school, or worry about Issa embarrassing him once again. He was cool. For once it seemed like everything was fine and calm and completely devoid of doom.

He was wrong.

Chapter 14

New Kid

Aunt Sabrina dropped Issa and Theo off at the curb in front of the school.

"Come straight home after school today."

"I got basketball tryouts," Theo countered.

"No, no," Aunt Sabrina said, shaking her head. She was barefaced, no makeup, wearing cuffed overalls, and she'd just pulled her hair into a sloppy turban she'd made from old Bethune-Cookman T-shirts. It wasn't like her to be out like that. It wasn't like her to get up that early at all. "Um . . . ask if you can come another day. Not today. I—need to check something."

"Did you get a vision?" Issa asked.

"J-just do what I tell you, okay. Straight home!"

Aunt Sabrina slammed the car door and peeled out of

the parking lot like she was being chased. Theo and Issa stared at each other.

"What was that all about?" Issa said, not really expecting anyone to answer.

"Maybe she's got a date?"

They both swung around. It was Romare.

"Yo, what you doing here?!" Theo said as he dapped him up.

Romare shrugged. "Transferring. My mom talked to your aunt about the school. Guess she liked it."

Theo could see Romare's mom talking with the school principal in front of the building.

"Who's that?" Romare asked, and Theo looked down to see Rupert sticking his head out of his pocket.

"My snake."

Romare stuck out his finger to see if Rupert would lick it, and they fell into a conversation about the difference between public school and homeschool, which they'd both hated but all Bikin kids had to suffer until they could hide their powers. Then they talked about their matching obsessions with dinosaurs in the first grade and then at lunch it was Beats headphones vs. Apple AirPods. Theo had never really talked this much in his life, but maybe that was because he didn't have someone to talk to. Someone just like him, but not. By the time school was over, he'd forgotten what his aunt had told him. Well, he didn't really forget; he just put it out of his mind like the dead woman on the bleachers watching them line up for tryouts.

"You made it!" Frank said. He walked Romare and Theo over to the rest of the guys to introduce them. "Tryouts aren't really about cutting people. At least that's what my older brother says. It's like Coach just wants to see how much abuse you can take or if you've got grit or whatever."

Romare and Theo exchanged a look, but they suited up anyway. They didn't call drills suicides for nothin'. How bad could it be?

There were guys much better than Theo, but then again, he wasn't the worst on the court. The stands were mostly empty, save a few girls who came to watch 'cause they had nothing better to do and a few parents, including Ms. Carlisle, Romare's mom, who was louder than anyone. Not that she needed to do anything to stand out. She was tall, with waist-length black hair that matched her pitch-black skirt suit and black lipstick. She also wore a black fedora tilted to the side. She was pretty, too, which seemed to distract the dads in the audience—the coaches too. Maybe it was her smile that canceled out every sign that she was highly dangerous.

It was full dark by the time Theo walked in the house, still sweaty and stinking from drills. As soon as he stepped across the threshold, he met a slap across the face.

"Disobedient boy!" Aunt Cedella screeched before squeezing him in an airtight hug. Then she gripped his arms so hard her nails dug into his skin as she looked him over head to foot.

"Where were you?"

"At basketball tryouts."

"Why didn't you answer your phone?" Aunt Ionie yelled from the kitchen.

Theo hadn't looked to see how many missed calls he had. He'd turned off his phone so he wouldn't have to explain why he'd deliberately disobeyed Aunt Sabrina. Still gripping his arm, Aunt Cedella dragged him to the kitchen table and shoved a piece of paper in his face.

It was a picture of him, as large as the Hulk, towering over their house. He was bruised and bleeding, and his fist crashed down into the roof. There were other pictures too, some in pencil, chalk, oil pastels. In every one he was destroying the Tatterly house in a fire, peeling back the roof.

"This doesn't make any sense," Theo whispered, horrified.

"And Great-Aunt Trudy Anne told New Nana that the ghosts are restless. Somebody's been stealing souls," Aunt Ionie said, her arms folded firmly across her chest. "Probably some old demon somebody dug up or angered by accident. Not exorcising them—stealing them, especially children. The boy selling papers on the corner is missing. The peanut seller on the corner of Calhoun by the College of Charleston is gone too."

"I just saw Billy. I tried to exorcise him, but—" Theo stopped himself. Something had happened that day. He saw something, and he didn't want to make whatever this was worse.

"Who's Billy?" Aunt Cedella asked.

"The boy at the park," Issa interjected as she walked into the kitchen and snatched a clementine from the fruit bowl on the counter.

"All right. The Tatterly house is on lockdown," Aunt Cedella announced. "Nobody goes anywhere without an escort."

"But I got tryouts," Theo argued.

Aunt Cedella turned and attacked with a look that could melt wax. "You better be glad you're not grounded, period. If you want to go to tryouts, Issa or Femi will go with you."

"Why do I have to go? I got stuff to do too," Issa argued.

"I don't care! I'm not going to be worrying about you all while we've got real estate agents and city officials breathing down our necks again about the house."

"Cedella!" Aunt Ionie snapped. Aunt Cedella's shoulders slumped a bit as she blew out air and then rubbed her temples.

"Work it out. I've said what I said. You will follow house rules, or you won't leave the house. Got it?!"

"Yes ma'am," they both mumbled.

Now it was Issa's turn to offer up a look of death.

Femi walked in with a mixing bowl full of the dregs of cereal, his cheeks stuffed with Cocoa Crispers.

"What'd I miss?" he mumbled.

"We're on lockdown," Issa said.

"Oh no. No, no-no-no. I just started my internship with Dr. Mgazi. I gotta do ten hours a week if I want to apply to the astrological law program in Cairo."

"Theo can go with you," Aunt Ionie replied.

"Snot Boy?"

"Enough with the 'Snot Boy.' We are a family, and family looks out for each other. We are on lockdown, and that's final."

Theo flipped through the pictures on the table. Lockdown. Those could last for weeks. Weeks with Femi and Issa breathing down his neck, blaming him for everything. No. He'd have to fix this, and fix it quick.

Chapter 15
Night Marauders

A pebble hit the back of Theo's head just as he hit the sidewalk.

"Where are you going?" Issa whispered. He'd forgotten she liked to be on the sleeping porch late into the fall. In the summer, she'd move her TV out there too. She was still in her pajamas, but she'd slipped on her garden Crocs to catch up with him. She knew better than to slam the screen door on her way out.

The moon was high, so he could see her clearly. In fact, he could see everything clearly. Theo had excellent night vision. He wasn't sure if it was because he was a medium or not, but it was still a cool trick.

"I'm meeting up with Romare at the park."

"In the middle of the night? After we were explicitly told not to go anywhere alone?"

"I won't be alone. Romare will be there. I'm going to see about Billy. I got a weird feeling about this soul snatching thing."

"Even more reason not to go anywhere. And you know Aunt Cedella meant family."

"Then come with me. All of this is about Aunt Sabrina's visions. If we clear it up, then we won't be on lockdown and I won't have to suffer Femi."

It was a dare. Theo knew Issa couldn't resist a dare, and for all her faults, Issa was extremely observant. He could see ghosts, but she could see things even he overlooked.

"I'm not getting in trouble for you."

"It's fine if you're scared," Theo said. He began walking, knowing full well she'd follow.

The night was cool, and the wind blew the scent of the paper mill and the river into his nose before the breeze shifted and changed so that the scent of a late-night barbecue and fermenting beer replaced it.

"So you and Romare are like best friends now?" Issa asked.

"Jealous?" Theo retorted.

She laughed, but it sounded forced. "No. I'm the one who told you to make friends."

"Then why do you care?"

"I don't."

They came up on the park, and Theo was glad there were a few older guys still playing ball on the courts opposite the playground, though from where they'd be, no one would be able to see them. Still, their presence gave a small slice of comfort.

Romare was sitting on a bench, Nintendo Switch in hand like it was a sunny afternoon in June instead of near midnight on a school night.

"Ay, bro. I thought you'd chicken out."

"Nah," Theo said and dapped him up.

"Nice pajamas," Romare said to Issa.

She rolled her eyes. "Whatever."

"So, what do we do here?" he asked.

"There's a soul I need to exorcise. I tried to do it the other day and got distracted. Romare, you're on defense. You see anything move that shouldn't be there, send it flying. Issa, you're another set of eyes. I know you can't see ghosts, but you can see when things aren't . . . you know."

"Yeah, I know. Just hurry up. We're not supposed to be here," she said.

"What? Y'all on restriction?" Romare asked.

Theo didn't want to explain his aunt's weird superstitions, so he just said, "Something like that."

The screech of sneakers sliding on asphalt and the reverberation of the ball hitting the rim echoed in Theo's ears, and the creak of the swing that seemed to never really stop rocking back and forth. He focused on them and then tucked them away into the back of his mind so that he could open up his other senses, the feel of the supernatural. It was another pulse or a separate heartbeat that sped up in the presence of things not of this world, but another one, just unseen under the surface.

The moon got brighter for just a second as he stood still, and then he saw him, Billy, just as he'd been before. Theo felt relief wash over him. His aunts were wrong. There wasn't some ominous prediction to worry about; it was all just ghost gossip. He walked closer, aware of Issa at the corner of the playground looking right at him.

"Billy?" Theo called out, but the boy didn't answer. He had on the same brown corduroy pants and striped shirt, but he wasn't moving. Something chittered in the distance and howled. Theo jumped.

Romare laughed from his corner opposite Issa. "I know you not afraid of dogs."

Theo laughed too, but it was so hollow, it was barely worth pretending.

"That don't sound like dogs to me," Issa said.

"Billy," Theo called again. The barking seemed closer, but Theo ignored it. He walked around the swing set and stopped, his feet glued to the pavement, his eyes wide with shock.

Billy's body was there, but his face had a crater in it the size of a grapefruit. His skull was puckered on one side like someone had attached a vacuum hose and sucked out his insides. He had no eyes, and his skin, which was always pale and freckled, was white as paper.

Issa rushed over.

"What's wrong? What do you see?"

Theo couldn't speak at first. All he could see was the hair that was left behind blowing in the wind, and the black hole he was afraid to get a better look at. "I . . . I don't know," he managed to croak after Issa shook his arm.

"What do you mean you don't know?"

"I don't know, Iss!" he snapped, and then what had been the distant sounds of barks became an extremely close sound of a very large dog growling.

They both turned and met the eyes of a hound. He couldn't categorize it as a dog, because it was bigger than that, almost as large as a horse. He pushed Issa behind him, for all the good that would do. The hound snapped its jaws, and white foam flew past them both. Its breath smelled like day-old raw meat left in the trash bin, and its fur was missing in patches, where raw and bloodied skin were exposed. Its eyes glowed red, and Theo tried to remember his one cursory lesson in telekinetics. But he couldn't think of the spell, couldn't think of the words and then . . .

"Run!" Romare shouted. The dog was upended, tail over paw, into the bushes nearby. Theo dug into his pockets for warding salt, but he didn't slow to turn around. Romare was right next to them, but he wasn't fast enough. The hound landed on his feet and pounced, clamping down on Romare's sneaker. He yelled.

Issa, more underdressed than the boys and in garden slippers at that, was already up the street. Theo turned. This time he was quicker. He whistled like Uncle Mack taught him and tossed the warding salt. The granules rode the wind and went straight for the beast's eyes. It howled, giving Theo enough time to help Romare up.

All three of them took off in the direction of the basketball courts, leaping over bushes and crashing into the iron gates, only to tumble into the middle of the court, totally disrupting the game.

With as much force as he could, Theo threw the salt in front of him and through the gate as the door swung shut. For a second, maybe even a breath, the silhouette of a man with fire for eyes appeared on the other side.

"Did you just throw salt in my eyes?" a guy in Nike shorts asked as one of the other guys stuck his hand out to help him up.

"That's what you get for being up past your bedtime. Scared of the wind blowing."

All the older guys laughed, but Theo, Romare, and Issa were too busy catching their breath.

Chapter 16
Dr. Mgazi and the Paddy Roller

Theo was exhausted from the night before and his legs were sore, but the smile on his face stretched his cheeks. In fact, he couldn't remember the last time he'd smiled so wide. Last night was—fun. Much more fun than Aunt Ionie's interrogation that morning. She'd stared at him for a full minute before he left for school, and he was almost sure that she could see what had happened the night before. When she reached a hand up to his forehead, he flinched, only for her to pull a strand of dog fur from his scalp.

"What's this?" she asked.

Theo played it off. "I don't know!" he squeaked while his stomach tied itself in knots. She squinted at him and rolled the fur between her fingers.

"Mm-hmm," she replied, and then turned her back on him. It meant they were done talking, but she wasn't satisfied with his responses to her questions. He knew then things had to be bad with the house, because Aunt Ionie never let anything go. There had been another couple sniffing around that morning. At least these people didn't get out of their car; they just stared up at the house from the curb and took pictures as Theo and Issa piled into the car for school, as if Theo's family were just part of the decor. Aunt Ionie flicked her wrist, and their phone flew out of the window and cracked on the sidewalk. Issa laughed so loud that orange juice shot out of her nose.

Frank tossed the ball to Denzel, who dribbled and then immediately passed it to his twin brother, Blair.

"I got you!" Theo yelled as he sprinted downcourt. He was open. Romare was on the opposing side that day, and even though they were friends, he didn't cut him any slack. "Kinda slow today," he teased.

Theo faked right and then jumped left, snatching the ball out of the air. He took two steps right and shot.

Down he went. The coach blew his whistle.

"Foul!"

Blair helped Theo to his feet.

"Free throw time," he said.

Theo nodded. "I hate free throws."

"Well, you're in luck, Tatterly," the coach said, "'cause we're out of time. Good hustle today. That's the kind of dedication I want to see every day. Go home. Wash your pits, and for God's sake, bring clean socks tomorrow. The locker room smells like something died, and we're only in tryouts."

"Yeah, Blair. I'd cosign, but you don't even wear socks," Olu teased as he peeled off his T-shirt.

Blair, whose overbearing grandmother had named him after Blair Underwood and his twin brother after Denzel Washington, threw Olu two middle fingers. "I don't like how they feel on my feet."

"Well, we don't like how yo shoes smell on your feet. Bruh, you *rank*!" Frank teased.

Romare shook his head. "Stank," he chimed in.

Theo followed with "So funky, make ya mind go blank."

The whole team turned to look at him, seeming surprised at how he'd joined in the teasing, probably because he usually kept his mouth closed. For a second Theo thought he'd misstepped. Maybe he shouldn't have said anything at all, or maybe he hurt Blair's feelings and now everyone hated him. But then everybody burst out laughing, even Blair.

"Oooooooh! He got you!"

"The funk rose Theo's voice from the dead."

"Blair's funky feet got superpowers!"

They all teased and laughed. Some hit the showers, but most just changed back into their school clothes so they could get out quicker.

Coach Lattimer patted Theo on the back as he made his way out of the locker room. "Good focus out there. Most kids think good game play is all physical. It's not. It's mental too."

Theo didn't have a response. Now that the heat of play was over, he was back to thinking about the supernatural again. They'd just barely missed that attack from the hound and he wondered what it had to do with him, Billy, the problems with the house, and the hag. He knew they were connected, but how?

Femi had spent practice on the edge of the bleachers with his computer and was waiting in the parking lot as soon as practice ended. Aunt Ionie had picked up Issa a little early so they could both get their hair braided. They probably wouldn't be back until everyone else was in bed. Theo slipped into the back seat. Femi didn't like him riding in the front.

"What kind of demon can eat a soul?" Theo asked Femi, half expecting him to ignore him like he always did when he was pissed at him.

"Don't be stupid. The aunts are just overreacting. Only a god can strip a soul from its body."

"Not from the body. Strip the soul from a ghost."

"That doesn't make any sense. A ghost is a soul."

"No. That's what I thought too. You know anything about demon dogs?"

"What are you talking about?" Femi asked, but Theo didn't answer. He'd have to explain what he saw and where he'd been, and even though it was against Femi's personal code to snitch, he didn't want to admit to anything right now.

Dr. Mgazi had an office above a knitting shop called String of Purls. He was a short man with a round face and close-cut graying hair. His pants were too long, and his shirt needed another pass with the iron, but he still wore a bowtie with a little cowrie shell sewn into the middle.

"Ah, Femi. Who's this?"

"This is my cousin Theo. He's gonna come with me for a little while. He'll just do his homework. I promise he'll be out of the way."

"Oh, that's no trouble."

Dr. Mgazi stuck out his hand and Theo shook it, noticing the slayer clan tattoo on the inside of his wrist.

"You're a slayer?" Theo asked, and then remembered his manners. "I—I'm sorry. I didn't mean to."

Femi blew out a puff of air, irritating Theo to no end. Dr. Mgazi laughed.

"Oh no. It's all right, my boy. Quite all right. I come from a long line of slayers. At one time I did pursue it, but my focus is the law now."

"What kind of creature can eat a soul?"

Femi threw up his hands. "Sir, please ignore him. We have work to do."

"Femi, Femi. I don't often get to think about these matters any longer. I welcome the question. Reparations work can be all-consuming."

Theo scrunched his eyebrows. "Reparations?"

"Femi hasn't told you about our work?"

Theo shook his head.

"Femi, you should be ashamed. I am suing the Global Coven on behalf of the descendants of enslaved American Bikin, or witches, as they might call them. It is against the written laws in the Book of Ages to enslave or participate in the enslavement of another witch or warlock. Furthermore, if aid is requested, members of the coven are bound to give it."

"The Global Magic Authority argues that enslaved peoples weren't members of the coven then," Femi said over his shoulder as he set up his computer at the table nearest the window.

"But I have found evidence that when Mansa Musa went on his pilgrimage to Mecca, members of his retinue joined the coven and were listed in the membership scrolls as members of the kingdom of Africa."

Dr. Mgazi dragged out the last syllable with a flourish, as if this were something very impressive.

"But there is no kingdom of Africa," Theo replied.

"Yes, but they did not know that. They assumed that Mansa Musa had conquered the entire continent. Not a horribly ridiculous idea, given how wealthy he was. It was easy to assume and their own mistake, but because they assumed that all inhabitants of Africa were members of the coven, then those inhabitants deserve full rights that all members enjoy."

"Cool."

"Very cool," Dr. Mgazi agreed.

"So what would we get, like cash? Stocks or mules or something?"

"Nothing so gauche as that."

Femi peeked over his monitor. "Priority and unrestricted access to the forbidden scrolls in Turkey. Those who knowingly enslaved Bikin would have to grant land."

"It requires meticulous review of genealogical records. That's why I need Femi's help. Now back to your original question about soul eaters. Do you mean Bikin who make zombies?"

"No. I mean something that could snatch the soul from a ghost and just leave his . . . uh, not his body but, uh—"

"His shell?" Dr. Mgazi finished for him.

Theo nodded.

Femi closed his laptop. He was listening.

"And you saw this?" Dr. Mgazi asked.

Theo opened and then closed his mouth, then shook his head. "Hypothetically?" he said, his voice rising, even though he hated when it did that.

Dr. Mgazi laughed. "Okay. Hypothetically. What would this shell look like?"

"Like an old snakeskin, but in the shape of a person. Empty on the inside."

"Assuming you've never been to the interior of the Congo or Siberia in the dead of winter, I will assume you mean something that could do that here in Charleston. In that case, there are only two options. One is a supernatural astrological event where the moon in our universe aligns with three moons in three other galaxies outside the proven universe and the dead rise and oceans boil as new gods establish themselves on Earth. Seeing as how the oceans are still the same temperature as they were yesterday, the other option is most likely: the Paddy Roller."

Femi laughed. "The Paddy Roller is a folk tale. New Nana used to tell me those stories so I wouldn't go wandering away from my mom at the Night Market."

"Did you say Paddy Roller or Pat Roller? My great-aunt said something about one once," Theo chimed in.

"It's most likely the same. Names can change slightly as they are passed on orally. Where do you think folk tales come from? There is always an element of truth in old wives' tales, and new demons rise every day as the cruelty of man grows. The Paddy Roller, or Patty Roller or Pat the Roller is a demon born from cursed slave catchers. He travels with two hellhounds, sometimes on horseback, and carries a bloody whip at his hip. He has torches for eyes, and his skull is bloody underneath his black hat."

"Not a kiyoberu?" Theo asked.

"My, my, you are inquisitive. I caught a kiyoberu once in my early training in Cairo, but no, a kiyoberu isn't strong enough to eat a soul, and I doubt she'd have a reason."

"Why does the Paddy Roller eat them?"

"He's consumed by greed. In life, his thirst for torture and grief led him to catch people for profit. In death he is still hungry. We are not just flesh or even soul, but energy. It's the essence of life that he seeks. He is the worst of creatures. There is no peace, no rest, no hope of escape if the Paddy Roller gets you."

"So there's nothing that can beat it?" Theo asked.

"Now, I did not say that. Nothing is invincible."

"So it can be killed?"

Dr. Mgazi scrunched his shoulders. "*Killed* is such an odd word to use in this circumstance. This is a creature born of curses. Whispered prayers and dying breaths. Transitional energy. It is the darkness made solid, so to speak, the bitterest of bitter magic. You would need to know who conjured the demon. A whole host of things. It's very interesting stuff. I once thought about a career in folklore, if not slaying directly. Less violence, you know. I am a humble soul. I have a very quiet nature. I do have an old colleague who works at Paper and Pin on Rutledge. I'm sure he knows more."

Theo looked at Femi expectantly, asking a question without opening his mouth. He got folded arms in response.

"Can we get back to our real work and leave the fairy tales to preschool teachers?"

Dr. Mgazi shook a finger at Femi. "This is why I need you. Always on time. Always on the ball. Let's get to it."

Femi and Dr. Mgazi began going over strategies and pulling books off the shelves. The printer booted up and began to spit out paper. It was all business, and Theo was left to his own thoughts.

Chapter 17

Tryouts

Aunt Sabrina was in the stands talking with Romare's mom. Aunt Sabrina didn't look any better than she had the last time he saw her, and he was starting to get worried, but she did manage to put on some color today with her mango-colored headwrap. She'd also covered her arms from pinky to shoulder with protective adinkra symbols written in henna. Every time she looked at him, her mouth puckered like she was thinking hard enough to hurt.

Romare passed the ball so quickly Theo almost missed it. "Get your head in the game!"

Theo sprinted to the paint and dipped low into an ankle-breaker dribble. Defense was on him hard, and at first he didn't have a clear shot, but he was quick and then he shot.

"Kobe!"

The ball bounced off the rim and was snatched out of the air. Coach Lattimer blew his whistle, and he was called to a huddle.

"What's up with you?" Frank whispered as they passed each other on the court. They were playing on opposing sides for the tryouts, a paper number pinned to each of their jerseys.

"I'm good," Theo lied.

"Get better, or they gone cut you," Frank offered, and lightly punched him in the arm. Theo nodded and kept on jogging.

"Hustle, Tatterly," Coach called out. Theo ran faster and took a knee with the rest of the guys.

"Any luck?" Theo asked Romare. They hadn't had a chance to talk before dressing and hitting the court.

Romare shook his head. "My mom isn't taking me anywhere. She said she's got work, and then she wanted to know why I wanted to go to a bookstore. Started asking all these questions I didn't have the answers to. She's been . . . I don't know. Weird, lately. It's a no-go. You?"

"Femi . . . he's . . ."

"Just ask him. All he can say is no, and then we can think of something else or nothing at all. I say we just let it lie."

Theo couldn't explain why that was an absolute impossibility. His aunt had had a vision, and until it came through or she was given a counteracting vision, life was going to be like being on house arrest. Romare didn't know how much worse it could be. Chaperone escorts was just step one. Next was ritual cleansing, and then full lockdown where no one goes into or out of the house. Not to mention that little message of doom Mr. Charlie gave him. No, he needed to find out more about the Paddy Roller and if it had anything to do with the hag. Something the little ghost girl had mentioned about a man with dogs kept eating at him.

Coach went over a play Theo couldn't really understand, but it didn't matter, 'cause he was benched. He worried about it for a minute but then let it go, because the assistant principal ran in and pulled all the teachers to the side. By the looks on their faces, whatever was up was bad. For a moment Theo hoped it was a burst pipe or something and school would be canceled. He was about to say as much when Coach Lattimer blew his whistle.

"Practice is canceled. They've found Philip Gray."

Theo looked up into the stands to find Aunt Sabrina, but she was already right behind him, her hand gripped around his arm.

When Aunt Sabrina pulled up to the house, Theo could smell the spice in the air. As soon as he stepped into the house, Uncle Mack had him in a headlock.

"Uncle Mack!" Theo groaned, but he secretly loved it. His aunts could be a bit soft with him, and Femi avoided him like he had a disease sometimes, so it was fun to roughhouse when he could.

"Heard you ballin' now. How's it going? We gettin' a ring this year?" Uncle Mack asked.

Theo shook his head. "Coach says I gotta work on getting my head in the game."

"Have you been meditating?" Aunt Ionie asked. He nodded. She came over and cupped his chin in her hand, and the light glinted off the rhinestones embedded in the nails on her thumbs.

"Tell me the truth."

"No."

"I need you to meditate every day. It's like brushing your teeth. It'll help you keep your soul attached to your body. It's important for a medium."

Theo nodded and rolled his eyes. Aunt Ionie had tried to teach Issa, but she couldn't sit still. She had a restless spirit.

"You smell like fire," Theo said as she planted a huge kiss on his cheek that she then rubbed off with her thumb.

"There was an incident up at the school in one of the kitchens. They say it was an electrical fire, but I think it might be magical. They say there's an old chemistry professor whose ghost likes to roam around, and Great-Aunt Trudy Anne sent Sabrina a message to shore up our protection charms at work," she said as she moved to Issa to plant a kiss on her cheek as well.

"And hello to you too, Miss Purrkins," she cooed to Issa's cat, who had slunk into the kitchen on their arrival.

Issa beamed and picked up her kitten.

"Always good to have a watchful cat around."

"And a snake!" Issa replied.

"True, even better. Nana Mae had protection on the mind too. Now come on and get some of my famous jerk crab legs since Uncle Mack seems to be gracing us with his presence once again."

Theo didn't have to be told twice.

"Sabrina. What's got you all scrunched in the face?" Ionie asked.

Sabrina told her all about Philip Gray and her vision.

Ionie pursed her lips. "Now, that doesn't seem like it's connected to anything going on up in here. And we've got enough going on with this property situation with the city. We'll pray for the child's family, but I think we're fine."

"You didn't see what I saw, Ionie," Aunt Sabrina argued.

"Okay, okay. Show me," Ionie said in a soft voice, and she let her sister lead her to her studio behind the house.

"She don't look good," Uncle Mack remarked as Theo pulled a butter cookie from the cookie jar.

"Wait, is there anything in this?" Theo asked Aunt Cedella. She shook her head.

"I don't have to put a conjure on my cookies to get you to stay in line."

Aunt Cedella pulled two cookies out of the jar herself and handed them to Uncle Mack before setting her eyes firmly on Theo. "It's the stress. If you just sat home like I told you, we wouldn't have these problems. I'd feel much more comfortable with you at Raheem's than playing basketball every afternoon."

"But I hate the Dungeon," Theo groaned. And he hated the bruises from gutter ball even more, but he didn't say that. It was no secret that the aunts, his granddad, and maybe even his often-on-a-mission uncles thought he was too sensitive and quiet for his own good. Soft. They thought he couldn't defend himself. They were wrong. He was never one to let anyone bully him or anyone in his family. Why was it so hard to believe that not wanting to elbow people for fun didn't make him soft?

"Femi doesn't have to go." His voice tilted to a whine more than he wanted it to.

"That's different, and you know it," Aunt Cedella replied.

No, he did not know that, but to argue would come off as disrespectful, so he ran up the stairs to take a shower instead.

After dinner he found Femi in his room, watching some gamer on Twitch.

"What do you want?" Femi asked as his speakers rattled with an explosion.

"I'll do your house chores for a month," Theo offered.

Femi crossed his arms and swiveled in his chair. "You want this pretty bad. Why?"

"I just like . . . folklore."

"You know I could just look in your mind and find out."

"I know, but you promised Auntie you wouldn't do that, and you like people to think you always keep your promises."

"I do keep my promises."

"So?"

Femi took out his phone and texted someone before he looked up. "Fine. I'm going on Saturday anyway. You can come. A month's chores. Thirty full days."

Theo stuck out his hand. "Deal."

Chapter 18

Paper and Pin

The car smelled like sage, and the seats were a little damp because Aunt Ionie had sprayed them down with Florida water to offer another layer of protection. She wasn't as committed to the predictions of doom as Aunt Cedella and Aunt Sabrina, but she still wasn't taking any chances.

"Everybody back by four. I've signed you all up to make sandwiches for the people going to the vigil for that boy," Ionie announced. "Don't give me that look, Femi."

"What?!"

"It's the least you can do."

There was a neighborhood meeting poster on the door of Paper and Pin. DON'T SELL GRANDMA'S HOUSE it read in large letters, followed by the hashtag #nogentinchucktown. Femi tried to open the door, but it wouldn't budge.

"It's noon. That's what time they open," Issa said, but Theo was focused on the poster. The meeting was being run by the Gullah Community Initiative, and the poster said they'd be discussing land rights, reparations, and defending legal challenges. Theo wondered if that was what Aunt Sabrina was talking about.

A guy rushed up and unlocked the door.

"I'm so sorry. Dr. Rollins was supposed to open today, but he didn't show."

"No problem," Femi said in a voice Theo had never heard him use, and then he nearly coughed when the guy wrapped Femi in a hug and kissed him on the cheek.

"So this is Darryl?" Issa sang. Theo just stood there in shock.

"Get out of the doorway, Snot Boy," Femi said, and that snapped Theo out of it.

"When did this happen?" Theo whispered to Issa as they followed the two into the dusty shop.

"Really, Theo. I need you to keep up, 'cause you don't catch on to nothin'. How do you even live?"

"Shut up!"

They followed Darryl into the shop, whose tall ceilings and hardwood floors resembled a Victorian tea room more than an antiquarian book shop. Bookshelves stretched toward the ceiling, and long tables sat in between the free-standing bookcases. Little apothecary jars full of white gloves sat at the ends of each table, along with magnifying glasses of varying sizes. All the wooden surfaces had been polished to a shine.

"Dr. Rollins!" Darryl called out loudly. Over his shoulder, he said to the group, "Sometimes he oversleeps in the attic. Weird, but I'm gonna go check. You guys can look around."

"Don't touch anything," Femi grumbled.

Theo clicked his heels and saluted to mock him, and then he breezed past, walking into the back hallway.

"This must be his office," Theo said more to himself than Issa, but she took it as an invitation to push open the door with the doctor's name on it.

"Wow! Looks like Granddad's living room," Issa said, gaping at the gallery wall of African masks.

Theo bounced out a beat on one of the vintage ceremonial drums, unable to help himself. The place even smelled like Granddad's house, all incense and Old Spice. Papers were strewn all over the desk, and the chair behind it was overturned. A glass of orange juice or something had been knocked over and had stained the rug. His heart skipped when he spotted who he thought was Romare's mother in the mirror. She disappeared as quickly as she'd appeared.

"Do you see someone in that mirror?" he asked.

"What mirror?"

He pointed to the one on the wall right next to Dr. Rollins's diploma in metaphyscial folklore from the University of Magical Studies in Medina. The frame was old and overly large. Theo squinted at the date.

"That can't be right," he said and pointed. Issa took a better look.

"Maybe it's his father's? This would make him nearly a hundred years old."

"I don't think Dr. Rollins left. I think something happened to him," Theo said.

Issa shook her head. "We don't know that yet. We can't jump to . . ."

Her voice caught on her own scream as something flew out of the jar of Murray's Pomade she'd twisted open. In an eerie mirror image of the model on the orange tin, the ghost's gloriously shiny conk whipped around her body like a tornado.

Theo was quick and spied a jagged piece of purple sugilite being used as a paperweight on one of the doctor's bookshelves. He tossed it at Issa just as the ghost had begun to sink his arm into her chest. She caught the stone and thrust it out like a dagger, sending the ghost reeling.

When the ghost finally stopped moving, Theo could see him clearly. Issa's chest was heaving with shock and anger, but that didn't stop her from snatching some quartz from a higher shelf in order to see the ghost for herself.

"You scared me!" she hissed as she gripped the stone. She was highly allergic to quartz, and the stone would leave welts, but she held firm.

The ghost, a reedy man in pinstriped pants and glasses, even in death, looked contrite. If you stood back and squinted, he looked an awful lot like Theo's great-uncle Nathaniel, Great-Aunt Trudy Anne's brother.

"I apologize. I'm sorry. I didn't mean . . . I mean, I would never. There was just . . . She's not here, is she? She took the doctor, and I hid."

She?

Issa looked like she was ready to fight, legs wide, fist clenched around the quartz stone. The ghost shrank in surrender, obviously afraid of her, of them. What could scare a ghost? He was already dead.

Theo quickly poured a vial of warding salt into his hands. "Don't move, bruh!"

The ghost's eyes darted from side to side, and then he stretched his neck long—really long, like it was made of chewing gum—so that he could look behind the two and into the hallway. Apparently satisfied that the coast was clear, he retracted his head, and it bounced back into place.

Weird, Theo thought. His arms were too long, too, like someone had pulled them out of place.

"Where's the doctor?" Theo asked, puffing himself up so that he looked taller, wider, and maybe a little more intimidating.

"She took him. Walked in here like it was a regular day and then attacked! I . . . I've got to hide. You gotta hide. Maybe . . . maybe you can help me," the ghost pleaded, and then he took a step toward Theo.

"Back up!" Theo barked.

"Why would we help you?" Issa spat. "You just attacked us."

"What? No. You came at me. I was minding my own business in my pomade jar. A great hiding place, by the way. Who invades someone else's hair products?"

Issa had the decency to be a bit sheepish. She *was* snooping.

"I wasn't gonna use it," she argued.

"Says you. Why'd you open it then?"

"Stop! Why do you think we can help you?"

"You're Bikin, like the doctor, but not like her. She had crazy eyes. She was unhinged. Wild. Dressed all in black, like Death come to collect."

"You're already dead," Issa countered. "What can she do to you?"

"So much worse. What am I talking to you for? You're babies. Kids." The ghost raised his arm dismissively but it floated down comically, like one of those blow-up dolls outside of used car lots.

"We know enough," Theo argued. "What's your name?"

"Cedric."

"Why are you haunting the doctor?" he asked.

"I'm not haunting him. We work together. I was fine, having attached myself to a set of my favorite writings by W. E. B. Du Bois. But the good doctor, a learned man and gifted man, found me at a yard sale, and I've been here ever since. We'd been working on . . . Are you sure she didn't send you?"

"No one sent us," Theo said, hoping he wouldn't have to spend most of his time getting this ghost to trust him. They didn't have time for that.

"Well, we'd been working on a special case. We were finding records regarding the Johnson family. They'd lived on my street during the riot."

"What riot?"

"Red! Red, red, red, red red. Red! Red Summer!" the ghost babbled, his eyes wild for a moment before gathering his wits to speak. He blinked, and then he was no longer a gibbering mess in pinstriped pants, but a soldier in an olive-green uniform, high boots, and a wide brown belt that stretched around his waist, over his right shoulder, and down to his left hip. He wore a cap folded like an expensive napkin that had a point at the forehead and another in the back. The dress change seemed to steady him. "Massacre. Riot. 1919."

He turned his head to the side so that Theo and Issa could see a small hole near his ear. A gunshot wound.

Issa shuddered and set her quartz down a second so she wouldn't have to see or hear. Theo thought about how lucky she was that she could just turn the ghost off, but then he didn't have to worry about ghosts taking over his body at will, so who was to say who had it worse? They were both vulnerable.

Cedric began to pace. "Bluejackets on leave from the naval academy got drunk and decided they'd murder any colored man, woman, or child they came across. Thirty-five dead." He paused. "Including me. More if you count the folks who didn't head to the hospital. I fought, but how much chance do you have against a thousand men? Seven families, prominent ones, on my street packed up and left for Philadelphia that very month. Some for Detroit. Left everything they owned behind. Bloody, just bloody. Blood, blood, blood, blood." The ghost began to ramble again. "Y-You—keep her away from me. She works for him. Turncoat! Wench!"

"Who?" Theo shouted, and the ghost pointed to behind them. They both turned to see Femi in the doorway, scowling.

"Did anybody tell you to come in here?"

"No," Theo replied, like he hadn't done anything. "The door was open, and we thought we'd wait."

"Did you make this mess?" Femi asked. "I did you a favor even bringing you two brats!"

"What? We didn't touch anything," Theo countered. Femi was out of line. He didn't need to jump to conclusions just 'cause he had a crush on the store clerk. But he was always looking for an excuse to pick on Theo. He always made it seem like Theo was in the way.

Theo scowled.

"Then what's in your hands?" Femi asked and snatched the sugilite from Theo.

Theo pushed him in response, and in a breath they were rolling on the floor. Theo got in a few knees to Femi's sides, but Femi had a few inches and about thirty pounds on him, and once Femi had him on his back, there wasn't much he could do.

"I didn't do anything!" Theo shouted.

"Shut up!" Femi growled.

"Stop it!" Issa yelled. She ran out of the room and came back with Darryl, who pulled Femi off Theo. In the tussle, Theo got in one good kick to Femi's shin, and he could tell it was a good kick—or a bad one if you were Femi. In return, Femi struggled loose from Darryl and punched Theo in the mouth.

The room stopped.

Blood trickled down the side of Theo's face. His lip was split.

"I . . ." Femi started, and he then rushed from the room.

"You okay?" Issa asked, reaching out her hand, but Theo flinched.

"I'm fine."

"I'll get some ice," Darryl offered and left.

Theo was glad he was gone. He didn't want anyone to see the tears in his eyes. It wasn't the pain. Not really. He let himself have the moment. One minute. Just a count to sixty and he'd suck it up and let it go. When he was done, he snatched the photo the ghost had been pointing to while Femi's back was turned and stuffed it into his backpack.

Chapter 19
And Then You Die

It was chaos downstairs. Aunt Cedella saw Theo's lip and erupted like Mount Vesuvius. She and Aunt Ionie were tearing into Femi, and if Theo didn't have an ice bag held over his split lip, he might feel sorry for him. Instead, he was just glad they ordered in pizza, because anything Aunt Cedella cooked for the next twenty-four hours would probably make you want to put a fist through a wall. Her emotions leaked into her food even when she didn't want them to.

"He doesn't mean to be like he is with you," Issa said.

"I don't want to talk about it."

"It's gotta be about his dad. Daddy said Uncle Yomi lost his last appeal with the council. He's not getting out."

"I don't want to talk about Femi or his jailbird dad."

"You don't mean that," Issa replied.

"Why don't I?" Theo said. He pressed a little too hard on his lip and winced.

"Fine. We won't talk about it."

They sat in silence on his bed while they stared at the photograph. Rupert's tongue stuck out as he crawled up Theo's arm.

"It's her, Romare's mother," Issa said.

Theo wasn't so sure. He turned the photo upside down and then held it away and then up close.

"She's younger, but it's her," Issa said again. "I'd bet money on it."

She pet Miss Purrkins and shook her head at Theo. "Hate to be you."

Theo sighed. Right then, he hated being him too. The woman in the picture with her arm around Dr. Rollins was almost definitely Romare's mother.

"Just text him the picture," Issa said.

"And say what? 'Is your mom working with a demon dog to steal children's souls? And by the way, we still on for hoops tomorrow?'"

"When you put it that way, it does sound kind of bad."

"'Cause it is bad."

Great-Aunt Trudy Anne appeared, her knitting needles and the same unfinished scarf in her hands. Theo stuffed the photo under his pillow.

"Clean up and go help New Nana change her sheets," she said, apparently oblivious to his split lip. "People coming tomorrow."

"What people?"

"House people, bank people coming to tell us what the house is worth. Not that it matters. Like you can put a price on the love in your heart."

"Nobody said anything about house people coming," Theo replied.

"Well, they wouldn't tell a child like you that, now would they?"

She was right, but Theo had to wonder why she was telling him if it was all grown-up business. What did Great-Aunt Trudy Anne know that they didn't? Probably something about the house being an amplifier. He knew it was connected to their magic, to the magic of all the first families. He thought about asking her about it, but she could be really secretive when she wanted to, and if you pressed too hard she'd disappear altogether. He'd done that once right before Thanksgiving two years ago, and she didn't appear again until Valentine's Day. If she was telling him about the bank people coming, then it was something he needed to know. He filed it away in his brain.

"Now go on and change them sheets," Great-Aunt Trudy Anne ordered.

"But I'm doing something right now."

"Well, Femi is indisposed," she said and faded.

"Whatever." Theo passed the photo to Issa. "Ms. Carlisle was talking to Aunt Sabrina at tryouts the other day. Ask her what she knows about her."

"Why me?" Issa asked.

"'Cause it's weird if I ask, and Aunt Sabrina's been looking at me all funny for the last few weeks."

"Aunt Sabrina still painting pictures of you setting us on fire and stuff?"

Theo sighed. "I think so, but I don't think she's showing anybody. Keeps her door locked."

"Aight."

Theo slid Rupert into the pocket of his hoodie and headed downstairs to New Nana's room. He knocked on the door before he walked in.

"Hey, Nana, I'm coming to change your sheets," Theo announced.

New Nana frowned, obviously upset with his bloody lip, but she swung her feet off the pillow they were propped on to the side of the bed so Theo could help her to her chair. An old episode of *In the Heat of the Night* was playing on the small television on her dresser. It was one of her favorite episodes, "And Then You Die," where Althea gets kidnapped. Her room was cluttered, stuffed with furniture that was too large for the space, and each wall was covered from ceiling to floor with portraits and pictures of her life. More than a few were from casino trips to Biloxi and Atlantic City. New Nana wasn't shy about her love for gambling. She said it was in her blood.

Theo took a seat in one of the plush chairs and watched a bit of the episode with her before he got started, not noticing that Rupert had crawled out of his pocket and wrapped himself around her arm.

"Why don't you visit me like you used to?" she asked, and Theo nearly peed himself with shock.

New Nana had had a stroke two years earlier that rendered her unable to speak. He hadn't heard her voice in all that time.

"Don't get all spooked out. It's the snake. Didn't know he could do that, huh?"

Theo shook his head.

"Snakes are very special animals, and this snake in particular. So? Why haven't you come to sit with me more?"

Theo shrugged. "Seems like you're always talking to Femi."

She chuckled. "Femi's special. We need to talk. He's very sensitive."

"Sensitive? Yeah, right. He's not the only one with problems. My mom abandoned me, and my dad is dead."

New Nana shook her head.

"You have a mother. You know Ro would die for you. So would Ionie and the rest. You have family. When your birth mama, Cree, showed up on our doorstep with you wrapped in her arms, you became their child. We were still reeling from your father's death, and there you were, the sweetest spoonful of him. You were the sun shining in our lives after he died in that war. You were always surrounded by love, and that has never changed. Femi, he started out in a little pool of love with him, his mom, and his dad, but when Yomi was arrested, that cup got dumped into this family ocean, and he's always found it hard to swim."

"I don't understand."

"Doesn't excuse his behavior, but we understand each other. Plus he's a wicked bid whist player, and a gambler can never refuse a good bet. But enough about him. Me and you are the only mediums in the house. I won't be here much longer. So don't let the clock run out on our time."

"Don't say that, Nana. I hate when you talk like that."

"I'm not gonna live forever, boy, and I don't want to. So what's on that brain of yours? Talk to me while you change these sheets."

She picked up the remote and paused the show.

"What's a turncoat?"

New Nana made kissy sounds at Rupert, who rewarded her with little flicks of his tongue in the air. "It means traitor."

Theo pulled off the sheets and dumped them in a pile. Traitor. Why would the ghost call Romare's mom a traitor?

"Were you alive during Red Summer?" he asked.

"Oooh, now that is a question. What made you think about that horrible time?"

"No reason."

"Mm-hmm. Well, no. I wasn't alive during the riots here. I was born a year later, but my uncle Caleb was there. Some silly fight breaks out, and it was like it gave all those good old boys a license to kill. Pulled men out of cars on the street to shoot 'em. I remember having a curfew and the abandoned houses on the streets in the Westside from the families who left. Your great-great-great-grandmother—we called her Salt Mother—had a time with the banks trying to push her out of this place, just like they trying to do with those folks on John's Island. Know good and well that's heirs' property."

She had gotten worked up a bit, so she took a moment to catch her breath. "I can't believe I never talked to you 'bout Salt Mother. She was a midwife, one of the oldest in town, and had helped birth more babies than anybody in Charleston County. Those women adored her. The men might have wanted to trick her out of her property, but their wives thought otherwise. You know, she wasn't Bikin."

Theo shook his head as he stripped the pillows and dropped the lot in an empty basket. He pulled a new set of sheets out from the trunk in her room.

"I thought all Tatterlys were Bikin," he said.

"No, every now and then somebody won't be born with it. Like you not being a conduit, and Issa not being able to see ghosts. But that don't mean she wasn't the most important woman in this family then or now. And if it weren't for her, I don't know where this family would be. She had her own gifts. She never once lost a woman in labor. Not once, and she must have birthed a thousand babies. Folks called her a saint. Your uncle swears that HappyTime grits used her likeness for their ad campaigns. You know, like the pancake lady."

Theo scrunched up his face.

"Salt Mother had skin so dark it shined, and she lived to be ninety-six without a wrinkle. It was just her eyes that dimmed."

"You talk to her?"

"I do. I can feel her around me. Not like a lost soul. Feels different."

"Aunt Sabrina had a vision."

New Nana waved her hand as Theo snapped the sheets and made the hospital corners.

"I heard. If this family falls, it ain't gonna be 'cause a little old you and lost paperwork, no matter what those little girls who call themselves aunties say. It'll be 'cause we forgot who we were, who we are, and who we s'posed to be. Here, take your snake. You 'bout done. Sit with me while Tibbs works this one out on my program."

"You seen it a hundred times," Theo said.

"So? I seen you a hundred times too, but it's still nice to see you. Give Nana a kiss."

He kissed her on the cheek and sat on top of one of the low bookshelves, thinking.

New Nana had a way of telling you what you needed to know without saying it outright. Sometimes she'd weave it in there, and you wouldn't know what it was till later. Like the time she was explaining why little boys didn't get their hair cut till they turned a year old, but what she was really telling him was why Aunt Sabrina couldn't cook. Round about, and then he got an idea.

"Put on my Mahalia Jackson CD before you leave. Ain't no evil Mahalia can't chase away."

Theo muted the television and slipped the old CD into the player. New Nana was right. There was something about the old gospel that lifted them, but he didn't have time for that. He had work to do.

Chapter 20
Gone, Baby, Gone

Theo softly closed New Nana's door and texted Romare.

> We still good 4 tomorrow?

> Can't. It's my dad's weekend. I'm gonna be on John's Island. Ask ur aunt if you can sleep over.

> I'll ask, but she gonna say no. Lockdown.

> Boooooo. Lame. See u at practice Tues. Congrats Point Guard.

> U KNOW! U too!

A brief smile crossed Theo's face as he took a moment to congratulate himself on his promotion to the team, even though nearly everyone made the team. The rumor was the coach felt guilty cutting folks after a kid went missing.

Theo poured himself a glass of orange juice and thought about what Romare had just said. John's Island. Why didn't he know that Romare's family was Geechee? Issa would say it was because he didn't pay attention, but Theo knew it was because it didn't matter. He just never asked.

> Is ur mom from John's Island too?

> Yup. Whole family. Like since forever. Why?

> No reason.

He closed the refrigerator door, and the flyer on the front jumped out at him.

DON'T SELL GRANDMA'S HOUSE. Keep Your Home. Keep Your Hope.

Tianna Carlisle, Romare's mom's name, was printed at the bottom. There were meeting times listed and workshops. One called Leasing Land Rights for Heirs' Property, and another was for a group therapy session for parents of missing kids. Theo thought to send a voice note to his mom. When she wasn't spelunking or climbing a mountain range or deep-sea diving in search of magical artifacts, she dabbled in real estate. She might know something about what was going on with the house and the bank and maybe even the wonky charm that was supposed to protect them but wasn't.

"You coming with me?" Aunt Sabrina asked as she breezed past him to get to the pantry. She looked better than she had the last time he'd seen her. She had added earrings and lipstick and was wearing her blue tie-dyed turban, but she still wasn't her usual self, and she wouldn't meet his eyes.

"Where?"

"To the Promise center."

Theo shook his head.

Aunt Sabrina said, "I'm gonna do an art therapy workshop with some of the grieving parents of missing and murdered kids. Tianna looped me in."

"I didn't know there were more," Theo said.

"You wouldn't. We send you to that charter school for a reason. You're insulated. But kids in the Westside have been going missing for years now."

Great-Aunt Trudy Anne appeared next to her on one of the breakfast stools. "A good bit of those kids ain't making it to the other side either. They ain't haunting their homes or their gravesides. Just gone," she said.

"Nobody told me that," Theo said. Aunt Sabrina couldn't see or hear Great-Aunt Trudy Anne and looked confused, so he told her what she had said. Being home meant he could translate for a ghost and no one would bat an eye. Aunt Sabrina nodded.

Aunt Sabrina took a deep breath. "It's just that they look like us, and some of them are poor. The news doesn't care about them."

More missing kids?

Theo turned the flyer over in his hands. "What does Ms. Carlisle do?"

"Umm. I think she's a real estate agent, but she told me she spent a year at the University of Magical Studies. She thought she might become a marine folklorist. I can't remember where she studied, though. Morocco? Madrid?"

"Medina," Theo said almost without thinking.

Aunt Sabrina snapped her fingers. "That's right. Medina. How'd you know that? Anyway, she gave it up. We actually ran into one of her old professors at a fundraiser at the aquarium."

"When was that?" Theo asked.

"Nearly a year ago. I was thinking we could do a fundraiser to bring awareness to the heirs' property movement there, and maybe pressure some of the politicians stuffing their faces with hors d'oeuvres to pay more attention to the missing children too. I remember 'cause it was right around the time Philip Gray went missing. Complete waste of my time."

Ms. Carlisle was a real estate agent, and she studied magical sea beings. Maybe the hag had something to do with the house trouble somehow?

"Did anything strange happen when you were there?"

Sabrina gave him a funny look and shook her head. "Not really, super sleuth. Nobody opened up the gates of hell if that's what you mean."

Theo didn't reply; he just ran up to Issa's room and burst in.

"Whoa! Rude."

"We need to go back to the aquarium," he said as he dropped a gris-gris bag on her bed. He'd followed Mr. Charlie's instructions and finally made a bag on his own. "That's for you. Extra protection."

Issa turned the egg-sized bag over in her hands. It had a thin ribbon around it so you could wear it as a necklace.

"I made it with some of the black salt Sadhya Auntie gave me, a strand of Old Nana's hair I found in an old brush in the attic, some of Aunt Cedella's rosemary from the garden, chipped paint from Aunt Sabrina's last vision painting, and some of Miss Purrkins's fur. Oh, and the bag is made from a swatch of my dad's Army duffel." Theo had also put a little dried scotch bonnet in there in case they came across any more demon dogs.

Issa slipped the small bag over her neck. He'd made a similar one for himself with a few key changes. His had cedar chips in the base salt and ashes from the letter his biological mother wrote him when she left him with the aunts, and instead of a bag he used his father's can of Murray's Pomade to keep it all in.

"Cool. So we going now?"

"You not even going to ask why?" Theo asked. It seemed Issa was all ready to run into battle. It was strange.

"You don't know what it's like to have someone exist in your body, what it feels like. It's like having two lives, two sets of hopes and all that swirling around the same place, and then when they're gone, they leave stuff behind. That girl at the aquarium was scared and lonely, and she needs her family. She needs to cross over."

"I didn't think you cared about final rest and transitioning and all that."

"Just 'cause I can't do it doesn't mean that I don't know it's important. So why do you want to go back to the aquarium?"

"I got all these pieces to the puzzle, but I can't put them together. Maybe if we go back we'll be able to find out more about the hag and how we can get rid of her. I think she's the one who took Philip Gray. I think she's behind all this stuff with the house."

Issa startled, prompting Miss Purrkins to hiss and jump down.

"You think we're that special. That's a leap."

"I don't think so. The more I thought about Philip, the more I remembered about him. He had this weird obsession with fish. He was in the Junior Marine Biologists Club, and he wasn't in school that day we went. The news said he would sometimes visit the aquarium. What if he skipped school like we did and she got him? What if all this leads back to us and that hound?"

"That's a big *if.*"

"Kids!" Aunt Ionie called from downstairs, interrupting their conversation. They rushed downstairs to find

Issa's parents, Tope and Thalia, in the living room, fresh from their flight from Japan.

"No aquarium tonight," Issa whispered before she ran into her father's arms.

The doorbell rang. It was Uncle Mack, and before anyone could say *lowcountry*, the grill was lit and Prince's full catalog was playing on the stereo system.

Later, Theo's belly was full of Uncle Mack's notoriously spicy jerk chicken and his lips were burning slightly in that sweet way that he liked. In a momentary lapse of anxiety he asked Aunt Cedella if he could sleep over at Romare's.

"Sleep over? Wow! I didn't know you guys had gotten that close. You've never asked to sleep over with anyone."

"He's never had a best friend before," Issa chimed in.

"Shut up," Theo said.

"Is this with his mom, Tianna?" Cedella asked.

"No, his dad on John's Island. His name's Fletcher Minton."

Uncle Mack laughed, his booming voice sending the wind chimes into a frenzy. "I know Fletcher. I been to his place on John's Island too. Good man. We served in the Marines together. Different units, but we kept in contact. Not too many Bikin in Korea at that time."

"Have you forgotten we are on lockdown?" Aunt Cedella pointed out.

"Fletcher got five Bikin nephews at that place on the water. All of 'em telekinetics and meteorologists. I saw one of 'em raise a half-ton boulder with a flick of his wrist while his brother called down a bolt of lightning to turn the thing into pebbles for their driveway. Mermaid pass on one side. Forest full of ninci nests on the other. Ain't a place for a hundred miles more secure than that one. Hell, I might go spend a few nights out there to recharge."

Aunt Cedella cut Uncle Mack a look that could have meant *I love you* or *mind your own business*. Theo didn't know which.

"And he's a good man?" Ionie asked.

Uncle Mack nodded. "One of the best. He'll be as safe as he was in his crib."

Maybe she was feeling sorry for him and his split lip, or maybe she was distracted, but just like that it was settled.

Chapter 21
Minton's Brood

A wasp nest is called a vespiary, and a nest of rabbits is a form, but a house full of Bikin is called a brood. There were no girls, no women, no aunties or moms or nanas at Minton's Brood on John's Island. It was on a track of wild land with a natural beach not fit for anything but chasing crab. It wasn't one house but three white cabins covered in gray adinkra set in a semicircle at the end of a dirt road. A horse stable could be seen around back. Theo could hear the characteristic warble of a turkey somewhere nearby, but couldn't see it. An ancient-looking dog raised its head when they pulled up to the brood, but it didn't move.

Theo and Romare tumbled out of Romare's dad's pickup and stretched in the muggy air.

"Home sweet home!" Fletcher Minton bellowed just as they heard someone scream.

"Aw, hell."

All three of them ran toward the sound and found four guys circled around an alligator, which was snapping at one of the boys.

The gator was ferocious, nearly six feet long with razor-sharp teeth. Its jaws stretched wide and lunged at a boy who looked faintly like Romare, but lighter skinned, with fierce gray eyes that slanted up at the corners. He wore a Tennessee State University T-shirt rolled up at the sleeves, jeans, and wading boots like all the other boys, and one of his hands was bleeding. He launched back at the gator and punched it dead in the nose. The animal shook it off and lunged, knocking the boy on his back, and then it closed in, locking its jaws on his right foot. The gator swished the boy back and forth, and Theo was aghast, wondering why no one was helping him. Instead, the other guys were rooting for the gator.

Mr. Minton stretched his arms wide and clapped his hands together, causing a small quake that knocked everyone off their feet except him.

"Now, I told y'all to stop all this foolishness! I ain't callin' for no healers, neither. Y'all too old to be carrying on like this. Tariq, get out of that gator and let Vernon go. Now!"

To Theo's surprise the gator opened his jaws and backed away. A second later, another guy who Theo hadn't noticed before got up from his seat against the nearby oak tree. He petted the gator on his head, and the ancient thing just walked away like nothing happened. The rest of the guys scrambled to get up.

"I hope like hell y'all got the oysters I asked y'all to pick," Romare's dad bellowed.

"We couldn't find a good spot," one of the boys answered.

Romare leaned over. "That's my brother, Vernon, from my dad's first wife. The one with the bloody fist. The animator, who can control animals, that's my cousin Tariq. His brother is the one in the Morehouse cap. His name's Jeremiah. And the guy with the USC gamecock tattoo is Baby."

"Baby?" Theo asked.

"'Cause he's the baby, until I came along, but he already had the name."

"Why I gotta come home to blood and bruises every time I leave?" Mr. Minton complained. He turned his back on the lot of them. "Baby, clean Vernon up, and then take a look at Theo's lip."

Baby slathered Theo's lip with some salve that smelled like the inside of a catfish's butt, but it was healed. Dinner was bacon-wrapped pork chops and candied yams. Theo and Romare stole a bottle of beer from his dad's cooler and snuck out to the horse stable to share their stolen goods. It tasted horrible—both of them squinted at the nastiness—but neither of them would admit it.

The horses didn't have gates on their stalls, and a brown mare with a braided mane came up to sniff Theo's head.

"That's Bree. She likes to stick close to home. The others like to roam around, but they usually come back here to sleep. There's a protection spell around the border of our land so they don't go too far. People can't see the land either. Otherwise they'd have tried to get my dad to sell."

Theo could see the mini mansions across the water. It was nice there, quiet and warm. The air smelled of grills from across the water, horses, and magic.

They heard footsteps, and Romare quickly chucked the beer bottle into a stall.

Vernon walked up on them and laughed. "Dad knows y'all stole that beer. He just doesn't care. You just better be up in the morning for oyster picking, and you better not be sick either."

"I won't."

"Yo, Theo. Don't let Romare get you messed up out here."

Theo shrugged like he didn't know what he was talking about.

"Yeah, aight. Play dumb. I guess that's what boys supposed to do for each other. So, you like it out here?" he asked.

"Yeah. It's cool."

Vernon gazed off in the distance, like he was drinking the air, and paused for a moment to pull out a cigarette. When he snapped his fingers, a tiny flame appeared on his thumb. Theo's eyes doubled in size, and Vernon laughed.

"I'll teach you how to do it. It's easy. Good for camping trips and stuff." He paused again, drawing in a puff of smoke and blowing it out so that the tendrils formed into a tiny smoke quarterback tossing a football. "I drive all the way from Nashville to come out here on breaks. You picked a good time to come out. Oyster season just started. Romare's mom just banished that hag."

Theo's ears perked up. "Hag?"

Romare nodded. "They've been building too much around here, disturbing final resting places for some old spirits. We had a hag that was scaring the horses and making it hard for the invisibility barrier to stay in place. She especially liked kids. They'd get spooked and run right into the barrier and knock themselves out."

Theo's mouth went dry. "Y-you said Romare's mom banished her?"

Vernon nodded. "Yeah, Dad called Ms. Tianna out to do it, 'cause he'd tried a banishment, but it didn't work. You know, if you don't do it right, you can call out other demons. He didn't want to take another chance at it. She's an orator. After she came through, we ain't have no problems."

Theo thought about that just as the sound of a buzz saw somewhere across the water sliced through the air.

The next morning they got up before the sun rose, and Theo had his first cup of real coffee. Aunt Ionie was adamant that children under thirteen never touch the stuff, but he didn't tell the guys that. They each piled into small grubby boats Mr. Minton had tied up on the water. Two to a boat. Theo and Romare had a boat to themselves, and Theo couldn't help but feel taller, older. They found a teeming oyster bed after an hour of looking, at which time the sun had risen, casting an orange glow on everything. The air warmed, and that in itself felt like its own kind of magic.

Theo loaded his bucket with oysters as the older guys teased him mercilessly. The fun didn't stop when he almost sliced his arm off trying to shuck them later so they could be fried, but he didn't care. He got enough to go alongside his grits, and that made the meal special.

"I love it here," he told Romare.

His friend nodded. "Me too. The city is mean, bruh. Out here, there's just us and the water."

"I feel that. Hard. It's like the city has too much heat. Too many souls caught up in it, and it's like . . . I don't know. It's like the ocean sometimes."

He thought about how school seemed to swallow him with so many voices and personalities swirling around him. How, increasingly, he'd catch older women and cops fixing him with icy stares when he wasn't looking. Some would turn away when they'd been caught, and others would stare him down with grinding teeth. The people constantly trying to buy the house, not believing he lived there when he opened the door. He didn't like it. It made him nervous, and it wasn't fair.

"Whoa, little bruh, that's kinda deep," Vernon said.

Baby threw a biscuit at Theo's head, and he caught it. "Deep as a tide pool."

They all laughed.

"You ever seen a mermaid?" Tariq asked.

Theo shook his head.

"Dark as river water at midnight," Vernon said.

"Eyelashes like peacock feathers, and lips like pillows you just wanna fall asleep on," Tariq crooned, licking his knife clean, and then he winked.

"They topless too," Romare chimed in, and his dad popped him upside the head. "Ow!"

"Have some respect," Mr. Minton chastised. The older guys tried to stifle their laughter but failed miserably.

Mr. Minton then launched into his predictions for the day's Carolina game, and the table erupted into talk of stats and all-stars, injuries and their collective ire over the current coach. Theo leaned over to Romare.

"Mermaids keep the memory of a place, right?" Theo asked Romare.

Romare nodded. "So they say. I dunno. I never really talked to them. We used to try to catch them coming out of the water, like folks do on those riverboat tours looking for dolphins."

"I wanna see one. I got an idea."

Chapter 22

Mermaids

The living room was crowded with the boys and a couple of local guys, so there was scarcely room for breath, let alone Romare and Theo. They waited until Carolina was up by fourteen to slip out. They figured that they could get a good lead before anyone would notice they'd disappeared.

"We'll have to use the paddles to get out onto the water. They'll hear the engine," Romare told him.

Each of them took an oar, and they slipped out into the gentle waves on a whisper.

They'd filled the boat with orange milkwort, whose flowers looked like flaming pine cones. Romare's great-grandmother had cultivated a patch of wildflowers just off the side of the big house. There were milkwort and wild snapdragons, thready blue mist flowers and plum-colored beautyberry.

"You gotta bring an offering if you want to see them. They take offense real easy," Romare said as he rowed.

"You think they'll show up?"

"I don't know. I'm not a mermaid. I'd show up just to break up the boredom."

Theo didn't think that made any sense, but he didn't live near a mermaid den, so what did he know?

"This is a good spot," Romare said as he pulled in his oar. He looked around them, squinting with his hand shading his eyes. "Looks clear."

He closed his eyes, held out his left hand palm up, and drew a circle in it with his pointer finger, round and round, until a tiny tornado began to form. It got taller and taller until it was nearly as tall as a man, but it spun quietly, controlled. With his eyes still closed, he called out to Theo.

"Toss in the flowers, a few at a time."

Theo did as he was told, gathering the delicate flowers by their stems and tossing them into the spinning wind until the entire thing was a swirling orange mass. Once Theo was done, Romare carefully set the tornado down onto the water, the same way you'd release a spinning top.

The tornado picked up water in a shimmering display of color and light. Petals and droplets spun out and rained down on them both, and their boat began to spin as well. A circular wall of water began to grow around them until it reached two stories into the air. The boat settled just as Theo began to feel like he might throw up, and he saw two pairs of eyes peeking out of the water, large and beautiful, with eyelashes like peacock feathers, just like Tariq said.

The mermaids were bald and had skin as smooth and dark as Tahitian pearls. They rose together with the bouquet of flowers in their arms, covering them from neck to belly button, where their skin faded into iridescent scales. They spoke in unison.

"Why have you come, last of the House of Tatterly?"

They said his name. Theo's heart skipped a beat as his mind tried to understand what they'd just said. Was he the last of the House of Tatterly? He was the youngest boy of his generation and the only one who was the son of a son. His father had gone missing in action in a special ops mission gone bad, or at least that's what he'd been told. His mother couldn't handle it and gave him up to the aunts, with Aunt Ro claiming him as her own. Most people didn't know the complicated story and didn't ask.

"I—" he croaked. He paused and cleared his throat. "I have a question."

They waited, and Romare nudged him. "Go 'head and ask then," he whispered out of the side of his mouth.

"I need to— Can— How do you banish a hag?"

"A hag. A witch. A demon," one of them sang and the other flicked her tail at her before she finished her rhyme.

"Hag. Tag. Lag. Brag. A demon girl steals breath to drag—a good child down," the rhyming mermaid sang before bobbing into the water and popping back up. "Mommy did a bad thing."

Theo was confused. This wasn't how he thought this meeting would go.

"A hag is a product of memory, a curse and a bargain. She is the demon born of demon. A god's lapdog. No one can banish a hag but her creator," the other mermaid said solemnly.

"A dog can sleep, a dog can bite, but the worst will come to boys at night!" the other giggled and began to lazily float on her back.

"Mudiwa, really?"

"Tsitsi?"

"Decorum," Tsitsi chastised.

Mudiwa flicked her tail and focused her eyes on Theo. "Aren't you a little young to battle gods?"

"What god?" Theo asked. Mudiwa just laughed.

"Dead boys tell no tales!" She laughed, and the water wall morphed to form a picture of Billy swinging softly on the playground with half a head. The image melted like a Popsicle in the afternoon sun.

"He marked you. In the playground. You, him, and the girl. He'll chase you. Track you like a lion who smells blood, and snatch, bite, snack on the bones of your entire family, last boy of the House of Tatterly."

"Then tell me how to beat him, her, whoever?" Theo yelled.

"A game! Let's play a game," Mudiwa shouted to her sister. Tsitsi ignored her.

"Well, tell me if the hag who was here stealing is the same as the one at the aquarium?"

Mudiwa stood still, a frown creeping onto her lips.

Theo calmed himself. "Please."

Romare licked his lips and gripped his wooden seat a little tighter. He cut Theo a look of stern consternation that made him resemble his dad.

Tsitsi spoke up. "Mortals trifle with gods, wanting their bidding done, but it is the gods who order the steps of the living. Williams's hag will eat and eat until her own creator calls her to heel. Turn away from gods, little one. Turn away. Turn away, or she'll grab your entire house, the mother too."

Romare looked at Theo. "What's she talking about?"

"I found a picture. I think your mom."

"My mom what?" Romare said, his voice getting thready and high.

The mermaid began to twirl and her sister joined her, clapping her hands.

"Excuse me," Theo called out to them, but they didn't stop twisting and turning. Soon they were going so fast that they were a blur of color disappearing into the water. In a blink, the water wall was gone, and the full light of day had returned. Theo felt more confused than ever. It *was* all connected. The hag, the hound, the people trying to get the house. How was he going to stop any of it? How much time was left?

"So you found a picture of my mom?" Romare asked as they docked.

"Yes."

"And she was with some doctor that went missing, and you think that means something?"

"I don't know. Maybe?" Theo said, feeling increasingly uncomfortable.

"Is that why you came here? To ask about my mom? To like snoop?" Romare asked.

"No, no! I mean, I knew about the picture, and I thought . . . I don't know what I thought. I had a really good time. I like it here. I . . ."

Theo didn't know what to say. It was all coming out wrong. He'd messed it up.

"It might be time for you to go home."

Chapter 23

Upended

When Mr. Minton pulled up to the Tatterly house, every light was on and Ro was standing in the doorway arguing with Aunt Sabrina, who looked like she'd been up for days. Ro was back early from her work trip. Something was wrong. Very wrong.

Mr. Minton looked over at Theo in the back seat. "Good having you, son. Hope to see you again."

Theo thanked him and closed the pickup door with a loud clank. Romare hadn't ridden back with them. Theo walked up to the house. Aunt Sabrina took one look at him and ran back into the house like she'd seen the devil himself.

His mother opened her arms and wrapped him in a big hug.

"I missed you."

"What's wrong? You weren't supposed to be back for two more weeks. Why are you here early?" Theo asked.

"Why does something have to be wrong? Why don't you go upstairs and shower and get ready for bed. You've got school in the morning, and you smell like outside."

"Mom, what's wrong?"

Her eyes rolled to the ceiling, and her shoulders sagged.

"I wanted to let you get some sleep first, but you . . . you . . . my special boy. Ugh." She took a deep breath. "New Nana's in the hospital."

"What?"

"The bank came by and assessed the house, and there were some legal setbacks. She just got a little upset about it all. She had a stroke. We don't know much, but she's getting the best care possible. We even called in a healer to visit from the Night Market."

"Why would you do that if it's a stroke?"

It wasn't common procedure to call a healer unless you were sure there was a magical affliction. Theo wondered what else his mother wasn't telling him.

"Aunt Sabrina isn't sure it was a stroke, but you know Sabrina. She can be a little high-strung."

But they still called the healer, so someone else in the house agreed that it could be something magical. Theo thought about what the mermaids said, and a lump formed in his throat. Was this his fault? Mentally, he made a list of warding and exorcism supplies he'd need to include in his magipack to be ready for whatever was coming. Maybe whatever was coming was already there.

"Now, don't get upset. New Nana is very old, and she's lived a great life. She might have more yet to live."

"But she might not."

His mother didn't reply. She just hugged him tighter.

Nana Mae's candles were set in each window, and Theo mopped the top floor with fresh Florida water and hung dried rosemary over each doorway before he went to bed, but that didn't keep the specter of death and misery away. Theo awoke to a house in chaos. Femi pounded on his door and then snatched off his comforter.

"Get dressed," he commanded and left, hopping on one foot to try to get his own jeans on.

"Why? What happened?" Theo managed through a yawn. He threw on a new paper-white Nike sweatsuit and slides. He was downstairs in five minutes, Rupert and magipack in hand. The clock on the stove said it was five till six, way earlier than he needed to be up for school, and his stomach dropped.

In his fog between sleep and wake he'd forgotten. New Nana.

Aunt Ionie fixed him with her no-nonsense glare. "Issa's gone."

Aunt Cedella slammed the cabinet closed and sucked her teeth. "She's not gone. She's just missing."

"She ran away," Ro said, reaching out to him. He leaned into the embrace and then pulled back sharply.

"She wouldn't run away!" Theo said.

"We know, honey. We think a spirit must have gotten in her window. The door cam at her house caught her walking right out the front door in her pajamas. She left the door wide open. She's not herself."

"I told Tope to double the protection spells on all the doors and windows," Aunt Cedella huffed.

"Cedella, please. They've been exhausted," Theo's mom countered.

"Hush, everybody. We're not blaming anyone. We're just going to go look. Ionie and Cedella, go talk to the police. Tope and Thalia are already scrying to trace her steps, but it's hard with two spirits in one body. Sabrina, you go to the hospitals and see if she's turned up there. I'll go to the school, and Femi, you take Theo to Tope and Thalia's."

"But we need to be out," Femi argued.

"I can't just wait—" Theo began, but Aunt Cedella slammed her fist on the counter.

"Hush! Sabrina's been in a fever of vision drawing, and it's too dangerous. You'll both fortify the protections on the house and wait there in case she comes back and that is *final*."

Theo opened his mouth to speak, but all four sisters clapped their hands twice, snatching his voice so that he couldn't speak even if he wanted to. His mother kissed him on the forehead in a kind of apology, but that didn't make up for it. He and Femi got in the car and rode to Issa's in silence, because they had no choice. Their mouths wouldn't move, even if they wanted them to.

Issa's house seemed hollowed out and abandoned, a ghost house. The silence spell hadn't really worn off by the time they arrived, so Theo and Femi engaged in a kind of sign language so they could divvy up the work of opening the windows, washing the floors, and burning sage to clear the house. Theo didn't want to talk to Femi anyway, so the spell was really convenient.

When he got to Issa's room, he hesitated at the door. He was unsure of what he'd find inside, but nothing was out of the ordinary. Her bed was unmade, there were clothes on the floor, and her plushies hung in their sling in the closet. She had LED lights strung across the ceiling in fake clouds made of pillow stuffing. It smelled like her too, a faint whiff of cocoa butter and lemons. Miss Purrkins scurried out from under the bed, and he reached out for her. A picture of Theo and Issa when they were four years old, in front of Granddad's house on the summer solstice, was on her nightstand. Theo picked it up and suddenly remembered what she'd said right before she went home with her parents.

That girl at the aquarium was scared and lonely, and she needs her family.

Issa needs her family. He closed the door to her room, turned on her TV, punched the volume up loud, and snuck out the window.

Chapter 24

Aquarium

Theo knew Issa was there, he just had to find her. It was an overcast day, and the construction crews were nowhere in sight. It looked just as it did when he and Issa came that first day: an abandoned site. Cranes and bulldozers were parked nearby and orange cones and caution tape surrounded the place.

He hopped the low fence meant to keep out trespassers. Miss Purrkins squirmed in his arms, and he set her down. Then he took out a salt shaker and laced the fenced area with a mixture of incense ash for smoke and pink sand for discretion, and he used clipped pigeon feathers to spread the mixture about. It was a quick hazing spell so that from the outside, all anyone could see was fog and steam. It wouldn't last all day, but it would last long enough. He knew that Ms. Carlisle was connected to the aquarium, the hag, and his house. And now Theo believed Issa shared the connection. It was time for action.

"Psst, psst, psst," Theo called to get Miss Purrkins to stop her explorations and come back over to him. He reached into the pocket of his vest and took a pinch of ground High John the Conqueror Root and dirt from Salt Mother's grave. He blew it into the cat's eyes and waited until they glazed over white. Then he whispered in her ear. "Call for Issa."

Miss Purrkins's ears twitched, and he whispered again. This time her whiskers shot out, and she began to meow. Her little kitten song was soft and mournful, the kind of sound you'd expect from a box of kittens being sold on the side of the road, fearful and sad.

Soon the wind shifted and an icy breeze blew past. Out of the rubble Theo began to see figures. Dozens of half-formed ghostly bodies rose from the broken concrete and steel bars. Girls. Boys. Crawling babies and teenagers. Some of them vacant-eyed and dull; others with mouths twisted in anger, a minority to be sure. Most of them were crying, some with just a whimper, and others calling out for the mothers, fathers, uncles, or grandparents they felt had abandoned them. These were the children of the sea, drowned and lost on boats and kayaks, pirate ships and slave ships. Sodden sons in khaki shorts and boat shoes, and drenched daughters in muddied sundresses. These were the hag's unholy collection. Philip Gray was caught among them, wearing the same Carolina hoodie he went missing in.

The fact that it was daylight didn't tame the fear and disgust roiling in Theo's belly. In fact, it may have made it worse. There was no fear in these spirits. They knew no help would come if they attacked.

Theo took out his phone and chose the song that he'd heard New Nana play a thousand times. The first piano chords of Mahalia Jackson's "How I Got Over" rang out over the rubble, just as a jackhammer sounded somewhere in the distance.

At first the ghosts kept slowly moving toward him, but as the song kept playing, some of them began to blink, shake, and stumble. Theo poured the special warding rub he'd made from the black salt Sadhya Auntie gave him into his hands and looked out over them, but something was wrong.

"Ms. Carlisle!"

Romare's mom's eyes were clouded over. Something had gotten inside her. Her usual perfect black outfit was covered in dust, her wig was ratty, and her stockings were ripped.

"You shouldn't be here," she said, but the words were delayed so that her mouth moved two seconds too late.

Romare tossed ash salt at her, but it didn't work. She wasn't a ghost; she was flesh and blood.

"Wake up, Ms. Carlisle!"

"I've come for what I'm owed!" she growled and kicked him in the chest. Theo hit the ground hard, and the ground rumbled. He scrambled backward and looked over at the children.

Spirits didn't often look this . . . decayed. They didn't growl or lurch. They talked. Sometimes they might just ignore you, but they weren't scary like these. Maybe he had done something wrong again, like what happened with Billy. His confidence slipped, but he didn't have time to worry about it. Ms. Carlisle was walking toward him.

"Use the activator!"

Theo looked up to see Issa on the roof, a mass of dark clouds forming above her. It began to rain.

Rupert wriggled nervously in his pocket, and Miss Purrkins hissed menacingly at the spirits, jumping on all fours, her claws splayed and ready for a fight. A crack of lightning touched down right next to Ms. Carlisle, and she lunged at Theo again.

"The activator!" Issa yelled again.

"That stuff doesn't work," Theo replied as he tried to kick Ms. Carlisle free, but he didn't have a choice; his salt didn't work. Theo pulled the blue-and-white bottle of activator from his bag and sprayed it in her face.

She screamed and reeled back, scratching at her face. He knew right then that he and Romare would never be friends again.

A boy in denim overalls and nothing else screamed; his lips curled back until his glistening purple gums revealed sharpened bloodied teeth. Mahalia continued to shout to heaven, and a girl in a long white nightgown began to scratch at her skin. Her fingers came away black with curdled putrid blood that didn't drip, but oozed. She opened her mouth and roared, her tongue a swollen blackened lump that unfurled like a lizard's as she howled.

There were so many, some clearly hundreds of years old, and others so new he could make out the brand of sneaker they wore. And then he saw her.

The hag.

On the roof of the aquarium she stood, her arms outstretched like a puppeteer toward her children, and Theo finally understood. All of them were under her control, even Ms. Carlisle. Nothing had gone wrong. Not yet.

In a burst of confidence, he closed his eyes just as the most able-bodied of the child ghosts was within arm's reach of him, sucked the damp riverside air into his lungs, and flung the bottle of activator out in a shower before him. A flash like lightning filled his eyes, and thunder rolled.

He was blown across the sidewalk, but when he opened his eyes a cavern had opened before him, ripped right into the earth like a small canyon. Blue light shot out, and dragonflies, bumblebees, and glittering iridescent beetles emerged from the hole. The sky opened up, and hail pelted the ground. Suddenly the chorus of the song got louder, joined by an invisible horde. One by one the ghost children were drawn into the hole in the earth, flocking to the light like water searching for the lowest point in the room, a flash erupting each time a spirit was caught.

It was a storm. It was a light show. It was everything in between.

There were dozens, and then in moments there was just one: the little girl with the bow.

She stood on the edge of the cavern, frozen in place in a way that none of the others seemed to be. Theo blinked, and the hag was no longer on the roof, but behind the girl, her bony fingers clasped around the girl's arm, digging into the flesh and turning her wavering form from a thin ghostly white to a healthy sun-kissed tan and then purple as it bruised. She looked nearly alive as she screamed in pain and was pulled backward, away from the cavern and back into the aquarium.

Theo rushed forward, but was stopped by the rapidly closing gap in the concrete.

"This is all wrong," he mumbled. He looked around for something he could jump onto to give him a bit more height. Someone had dropped an empty RC Cola crate near a trash can, and he rushed to retrieve it. With that little bit of height he could just make out someone's head peering out from the door on the roof.

Issa.

Chapter 25
Down the Rabbit Hole

It was dark in the aquarium, with just a few lights illuminating the fish tanks. Theo wanted to call out Issa's name, but he knew that she wouldn't, or couldn't, answer.

His heart beat wildly in his chest, and he could feel the sweat in his palms getting slick and cold. He had to give himself a pat on the back for remembering to put a little warding powder in all his pockets so he wouldn't have to dig it out of his bag. He pulled a pinch out of each pocket and rubbed it on his hands. They came away gritty, but they were protected. Rupert peered out of his pocket. The silence stretched into the long hallway like a bottom-feeding creature, just waiting to swallow him whole. His eyes adjusted to the gloom, and soon his ears did the same. He could hear something dripping in the distance. At first he thought that dripping water was normal, until the squelch of the carpet beneath his feet had him thinking again.

He moved faster then. Anything out of the ordinary is what he needed to pay attention to. Any movement or shadow could bring him closer to Issa. He rounded the corner, hating the sound of his squeaking sneakers. Anything and anybody would be able to hear him coming, and he needed to be invisible if he was going to stand a chance. The dripping got louder as he rounded the corner, and he had to slap his grubby hand over his mouth to keep from screaming when something rubbed against his ankle. He squeezed his eyes shut and then opened them to look down.

"Miss Purrkins?" he whispered as quietly as he could. The kitten looked up at him with wide eyes, somehow knowing that now was not the time to meow. Up ahead, he saw what was causing the drip. It was a large crack in one of the tanks. Something had bashed in the glass. Thankfully, the tank was empty, save for a few smaller fish that seemed fine in the shallow pools that were left. He chewed on his bottom lip as he moved slowly, his feet crunching the broken glass below him. Suddenly the entire building went completely dark, the small lights illuminating the tanks winking out together. He pressed his back to the wall and slid forward inch by inch until his foot caught on something. He kicked at it and bent to feel how big it was, and he realized it was a foot. Holding his breath, he slid his hand over the foot, the leg, and then the scratchy feel of soft pants. Issa's pajamas.

He fumbled in his pockets to find the black votive candles he had packed. He lit one, settling it in a pile of broken glass. He pressed his ear against her mouth. She was breathing. Shallow, but steady. He lit another candle and another, and then drew a semicircle of protection around her.

"Issa?" he whispered as he shook her shoulders. Nothing.

The candles flickered and turned shadows into people, and for a second he thought he could see her just inside the shark tank, staring at him, yelling at him. He blinked. His mind raced to figure out what would happen next. She was too heavy to carry on his own. He'd left his phone at the house so it wouldn't disrupt the magic, so he couldn't call for help, and he couldn't just leave her there.

He drew in a deep breath and crossed his legs underneath him, so that he was firmly in the circle. Whatever warding salt he had left he tossed in his hair and over his shoulders, and then did the same with Issa as she slept. At least he hoped she was just sleeping. Maybe some of the salt had gotten into his eyes, because again he could swear he saw Issa's reflection in the window of the shark tank, pointing at him and yelling. He ignored it and closed his eyes, trying hard to meditate in the same way that Aunt Ionie had tried to show him. He'd never quite gotten the hang of it. He didn't like sitting still like that, but he was desperate. There was only one person he knew he could reach out to who would hear him, listen, and even bring help. It was ripping out his heart to do it, but he couldn't leave Issa there.

Femi.

His ears were so open and attuned that he could hear the sizzle of the wicks in the candles burning and the click of Miss Purrkins's claws against the window as she pawed at the fish.

Femi, he called out with his mind. *Femi!*

He repeated the name in his head like a mantra until that second level of meditation reached him. The aquarium fell away, and his mind's eye was filled with bright light.

Snot Boy?

Femi's astral form appeared in Theo's mind. He was chewing on some beef jerky and holding a rake.

Issa won't wake up. We're in the aquarium. I need . . .

There was a groan in the background, a knocking that snatched Theo out of his meditation. He opened his eyes. He didn't even know if Femi had gotten everything he said. He peeled his eyes open. This time there was no mistake. It wasn't a trick of the light or a grain of misplaced salt in his eye. Issa was on the other side of the glass, but she was also lying next to him. He realized it was her astral body staring at him, screaming at him, and then running away.

"Wait!" he yelled. Then Femi's face was in front of him, mouthing words that kept going in and out.

The sound was in his head, but it was just as loud as if Femi was standing right next to him.

Theo said, *Issa's out of her body. She's knocked out, but I just saw her. I can't explain it.*

It felt weird to talk to someone he couldn't see, someone he knew to be alive, just not in front of him.

"Okay. Listen up."

You're hard to hear.

"Okay. There's a lot of interference. Sometimes dreams can muddle the psychic energy. I don't know how long I can maintain a connection. You need to get to Issa."

How? She's literally in a shark tank!

"She's not in a tank. She's out of her body, and the only way to help her is to get out of your body. You never should have left! But it's too late for that. I'll tell the aunties you found her. Listen, Issa can't be out of her body long. Her connection isn't as strong as ours, because she's a conduit. You need to find her and bring her back. Now."

But . . .

Femi said something else, but Theo couldn't understand it. He didn't try to reconnect. He knew what might happen if Issa couldn't get to her body. She'd die.

Or worse, she'd be disconnected forever.

Theo had never stepped out of his body before, but he'd read that chapter of the Book of Ages. It was simple. Deceptively simple. Just like whistling.

He closed his eyes and put his lips together to whistle. It took a few tries until he reached the right tone, the note that would detach his body from his soul. He blew harder, and then he stood and stepped just like he was walking into a pool.

Chapter 26
The Old House

At first the hallway looked the same, dark and silent, full of shadows, but when he turned he could see his body slumped next to Issa's, alive but sleeping. Miss Purrkins meowed up at him, fully aware of what he'd done.

"Can't pick you up. I don't have a body," he said to her. She meowed again like she wanted to tell him something and then scurried down the hall. He followed and realized she was leading him somewhere. There was a door in the hallway that went to another floor or outside, he couldn't tell, but Miss Purrkins trotted confidently through the crack. When he did the same, he wasn't in the aquarium anymore, but a house.

Light poured in from the windows. To his left there was a living room with sofas, and to the right there was a dining room, a large one with a few people sitting there who didn't seem to notice him at all. Miss Purrkins ran up the stairs, only to be picked up by Issa.

Theo ran up the steps, and his cousin snatched him by the shirt and dragged him into an open bedroom.

"Are you okay?" he asked. She nodded, holding her finger over her mouth.

"Be quiet, or she'll hear you."

"Where are we?"

"It's not just people who leave their souls behind. Sometimes it's a place. I think this house used to sit here way before they built the aquarium."

"That doesn't make any sense," Theo said.

Issa rolled her eyes. "You don't know everything. I'm holding an actual living cat in a ghost house. None of this makes sense, because we don't know all the rules."

Theo had an idea and patted his front pocket. Rupert stuck out his head, as real as ever.

"They live between worlds. At least, that's what I think."

She pet Miss Purrkins like she was drawing some kind of calming energy from her, and maybe she was. Theo walked over to the window and looked out. The street below was flickering in and out, changing with each second. In one moment, it was a dirt road filled with horses and buggies. Then there were stevedores passing back and forth with wheelbarrows packed with cotton and wooden boxes. The next moment there were shiny cars with wide bodies and chrome fenders that glinted in the sunlight. And then the entire scene was covered in smoke and shaking from cannon blasts.

"We're moving through time or stuck in time. I don't know. I don't think we can go outside."

Theo put his hand on the windowsill to get a better look out of the window but flinched when a beetle crawled up his arm. He shook it off.

"They're everywhere."

"Have you seen her? The hag?" Theo asked.

Issa nodded. "She's not a hag here. She's Fanny or Nanny McWilliams. I don't think she's seen me yet, but the house is small, and she seems to be everywhere at once. We won't be able to avoid her for long."

"Have you seen the little girl?" he asked.

"She's in the last room on the right. I was trying to make it down there when you showed up. I know you usually take charge of these things, but I'm thinking that if we can get her out of the room and then go out the front door, we might end up back in the aquarium."

"I called Femi for help."

"Good. Help is what we need. You gotta stop going it alone when you don't have to."

Theo didn't know what to say to that. He just chewed on his lip and took a moment to look around the room. It was regular looking, if old-fashioned. But Issa was right. There was a definite beetle problem. Their wings were an iridescent green that reminded him of the roaming peacocks in the Night Market. He could see one crawling on the bed covers.

Issa cracked the door so that they could both see out but no one would be able to see in. The top of Fanny's head, wisps of auburn hair, hovered on the stairs. She was talking to someone, and as she did her form changed: one moment she was the hag, waterlogged and decomposing, and then the next she was Fanny, clean and pink, well scrubbed and well dressed. Whatever had her attention, she had to attend to it, and she made her way back downstairs. Issa seized the opportunity and darted out of the room, narrowly missing Theo's hand, which lunged for her, hoping to stop her from doing something stupid, like running out into the hallway.

She was wiggling the handle on the door, and he could hear the girl behind the door, so he rushed into the hallway. With as much power as he could, he kicked at the door. It loosened on its hinges and the lock began to splinter. He looked over his shoulder to see if anyone was coming. He kicked again. With a loud clatter the door slammed open and banged against the wall. The girl ran out, as solid as any living kid, and Issa hugged her.

His thigh burned and his bones rattled, and when he looked over his shoulder again, he was staring into the tearstained, ragged face of the hag.

Fanny was gone. In her place the hag stood, seawater pooling around her ankles, the stench of rotting fish filling the hallway. Her lips pulled back from her teeth as her eyes settled on the little girl, and she wailed. It sounded like an air horn crossed with the death wail of a woman being bled. He used his arm to wave Issa and the girl behind him to shield them with his body.

Theo couldn't wait. He didn't have a choice. He dug into the deepest pocket on his right leg and pulled out a travel-sized spritzer of Issa's Everflame. He snapped his fingers, and a single flame appeared on the edge of his thumb. He spritzed one-two and blew so that the spray caught fire, and he was as much a fire-breathing dragon as he'd ever be. A blaze of red-orange flames engulfed Fanny's advancing form and sent a wave of fire up to the ceiling, peeling back paint and wallpaper. After the initial burst, charred black beams were left behind, and so was Fanny. The hag, dripping with river water, seemed to be immune to Everflame. Theo immediately launched plan B.

He rushed and landed a kick to Fanny's shins and a spinning back fist to her face. He didn't wait to register her reaction. He heard Uncle Raheem's and Coach Lattimer's voices in his ears, yelling from the sidelines. *Speed!*

He landed a straight punch to her chest. Instead of meeting muscle, his fist punched through the skin and bone like it was made of wet cardboard. He pulled back his hand, and bile rose into his throat as he shook maggots, bits of skin, and seaweed from his hand. A chill ran through his body as he readied himself for another blow, but the hag caught his fist this time and threw him backward. His head hit the back wall, and he saw stars. With a flick of her wrist, the hag picked up a chair that was in the hallway and threw it on him so that he couldn't get back on his feet. She laughed. Her withered form receded, and the old Fanny stood before him, a slight rip in her dress the only sign that she'd been harmed at all.

Theo looked over to Issa.

"Run! Get to the door!" he shouted, but Issa shook her head.

"Not without you!" she said as she tried and failed to move the chair from its perch on his legs. She shoved again, and the little girl was putting her weight into it as well. Something tickled his legs, and he craned his neck, trying to see what it was. He realized the hallway had become overrun with beetles. Blue, green, purple. All kinds. Theo's skin crawled, and then he remembered what his granddad had said about them.

Gods don't have to be large to be powerful.

The girls screamed and switched from pushing at the chair to standing on it. Theo swiped at the beetles crawling up his arms, trying his best to be as careful as possible, and watched as Rupert wriggled out of his pocket and slithered across the floor toward the hag.

As soon as he touched her boot, her voice boomed throughout the house, shaking the walls. The carefully constructed facade of the boardinghouse began to shatter, peeling away like a shed skin. The roof, which was still flickering with the fire he had set, fell away, revealing Charleston's night sky, cracked pipes, and a blinking exit sign. It was the aquarium.

Chapter 27
Paddy Roller

Something in the air clicked over and over, a ticking sound like tap shoes or the hands on a grandfather clock. The floor shifted, tumbling the girls from the chair and freeing Theo, but everything was at a slant now and a burst pipe from the real world showered water over all of them.

"This is our chance," Theo said with one eye on the girls and the other on the rapidly disintegrating image of the front door. The beetles shook loose from the changing walls and began to scamper in one direction, disappearing into one of the many holes in the cracked floor. Now the carpet was pulled taut over broken concrete instead of wood. "This place is falling apart. We gotta go when she's not looking."

Issa shook her head and pointed. They were tilted at an angle, and there was still a bit of sunlight pouring in from the window above the door of the boardinghouse. A cannon erupted; smoke filled the frame and shook the walls. A figure at the bottom of the stairs was undisturbed: a hellhound, its teeth glistening with spittle. The razor-sharp nails at the end of its paws clicked with each step as it started to move toward them. A rope, frayed and bloodied, was tied around its neck, like a leash with no owner.

Muscles in the dog's back rippled as it mounted the stairs and filled the hallway with its growl. Theo looked around for another escape, but there was nothing except rubble below him and behind him, and the giant dog was blocking the way out. He blinked, and a great wind swept through the hallway. The hound was tossed up and began to spin like a cyclone. Theo, Issa, and the little girl were blown into the corner as it spun and spun until suddenly there was a very tall, very gaunt man in its place.

"Now, now, Fanny. What have you done? You've gone and lost my treasures," the man said in a deep tenor. His accent was thick and gravelly, like his voice box was filled with rocks tumbling over glass. He had on a long black coat that grazed the top of his black leather boots. A shotgun rested in his arms like a baby, and nothing but two burning coals for eyes could be seen under his enormous felt hat. A gold bugle gleamed on the front of the hat, casting its own beam of yellow light into the gloom, and one side was pinned up, like his left shoulder didn't need any shade.

"None of this is my fault!" the hag screamed, pointing at Issa. "You broke the contract."

"Big mouth for such a little girl. You should talk to me about broken contracts when you fail to understand the terms of the deal you made or its results."

Theo looked around at the peeling wallpaper, the sodden carpet, and the crumbling floor. A shooting star screamed across the night sky as something blew up nearby. The entire house rattled as two buzzards settled themselves on one of the jagged beams left behind from the nonexistent roof.

"Tatterly boy. The last of the House of Tatterly. The fall of a once great name."

Theo, able to stand for the moment, stuck his chin out and spread his legs, taking up as much space as he could. He wasn't going down without a fight. In fact, he was determined not to go down at all.

"You came for us," he said.

"Of course we did. I've been looking for you for over a century."

"Okay. Let my cousin go, and the girl," Theo bargained. Issa kicked the back of his heel.

"Are you crazy?" she whispered.

"Don't you even want to know why, boy?" the man asked.

Theo shrugged. "Does it matter?" he said, keeping his voice level and his mind clear.

"I suppose not, but it might be nice for the record, should I decide to let that other one go."

"It's your time, demon," Theo said, liking the confidence in his voice. If he could keep the man talking, it might give him more time to think of a way out of this.

"So gracious. You see, I am not a demon. I have many names, but most call me the Paddy Roller."

Theo had been almost certain that was who he was dealing with, but he couldn't be sure of anything in this place. It was neither here nor there.

"I wasn't always like this," the demon said, waving his hand from his head to his thigh. "I had a home, a community, a name. Do you want to guess what it is?"

"I couldn't say. I don't know you."

"No, you do not, and that is a shame. My name is Theodore Bartholomew Tatterly. I guess that would make you Theodore the second."

Chapter 28
Family Ties

"Liar!" Issa shouted. Theo had the urge to do the same, but he couldn't get the words out. Maybe that was a good thing, because he wouldn't have been able to control his voice if he could.

"Tatterly Place became a gambling house after I retired from the slave patrol. I didn't have the body for chasing slaves anymore, even if I still had the desire for the money. Your folks cooked and washed and smiled in my face while they plotted and schemed to take my property for themselves as soon as I was called to serve in the War of Northern Aggression. I died for my ideals. I died a hero."

It was easy to see him then. The red coals receded behind gray eyes set above ruddy cheeks. He had a beard then, and a crooked-toothed smile, with ears that jutted out at the sides. He poked out his chest a little, and the outline of a gray uniform began to show.

"There was chaos after the last battle ended, and like many a restless soul, I made my way home one last time before I was to meet my maker. And what do I find, but your ancestor, Thomas, playing house under my name. I had no sons or daughters"—he paused to look at Fanny— "of the right kind to speak for the dead, so I did what I could and haunted them day and night until Salt Mother, frail as she was at just seven years old, made a deal with the wrong kind of god. He took her magic and made it mine, then he cursed me and her so that she could never make a deal again and I could never walk the halls of Tatterly Place."

Fanny, whose body mostly remained whole except for a ghoulish tear in her cheek that leaked dirty water and oily sludge, pointed at the man angrily.

"Uncle Ted, you did this to me. Terrorizing the coloreds made them curse the entire family. All I wanted was a child and the curse made sure I'd never have one," she whined as she reached toward the girl hiding behind Issa.

"She was just so beautiful, standing there on the edge of the water. Her parents weren't lookin'. They were neglectful. Selfish. I didn't mean to push her in."

Theo held out his arm to push the girls farther behind him and set his eyes on the Paddy Roller.

"We don't owe you anything. They worked and you never paid them. The least you could do is give 'em a house and never come back."

"You people always want more than you're due, and I mean to put a stop to it. This is about holy justice."

Two hellhounds with rotten teeth, bleeding gums, and mange eating away at their fur appeared at the man's side. Lightning flashed across the sky and touched down on the carpet, setting it on fire. Shadows danced across the walls as flames licked skyward.

Issa tugged on Theo's shirt and tilted her head toward a doorway behind them. The exit sign had been obscured by peeling wallpaper that was now crumbling to ash. He nodded slightly. The hounds barked at the noise and smoke, and Miss Purrkins gave as good as she got, spitting and hissing. After one last pat from Issa, she leaped onto the overturned chair and into the man's face, clawing her way down his chest until the front of his coat parted, revealing his dirt-covered chest heaving above a rusted Confederate States of America belt. He grew another two feet, and his coat peeled off like a tree shedding leaves. His boots

247

caught fire, and blue flames licked up to his knees. This was bad.

"I came for blood and paper, boy!" the man yelled and whistled. Out of nowhere a sheaf of papers appeared in the air, floating between them. "The original deed, modified and willed to my true descendants in Mount Pleasant, distant as they are." He whistled again and the papers disappeared.

Rupert, whom Theo had forgotten all about, slithered up to the Paddy Roller. Theo was sure he was about to get stomped, but something happened. The flames covered him too, but they didn't burn. Instead, the snake doubled in size, then tripled. His tiny innocuous tongue grew long and vicious, and his eyes grew as large as basketballs. His fangs dripped acid, which fell on the hounds flanking the man. The dogs whimpered and backed away as Rupert's growing girth circled the Paddy Roller and held him still.

The man roared, turning his head to the sky, giving Issa and the girl just enough time to scamper away. Issa pulled on Theo's shirt again, but he turned his head. He knew the Paddy Roller would follow. It was his responsibility to end it.

Theo raised his hand like he was in school as the demon wriggled in Rupert's grasp. The man coughed and regained his composure. Apparently, he was partial to formality.

"I don't want to put down such a magnificent creature, but I will," he said as his eyes rolled back in his skull and a piercing bird call rent the air. Theo looked up as a huge bird, part eagle and part dinosaur demon, circled the open sky. Rupert, who had been focused on the Paddy Roller, looked up. The bird was large enough to snatch and eat him in one swallow. He shrank and slithered back to Theo, who picked him up with care and slid him back into his pants pocket.

"Y-you're a gambler," Theo said. "A gambler can never refuse a good bet. How about a game? Me against you. Winner takes all. You don't touch my family or me ever again if I win, and if you win you get me. The last of the House of Tatterly."

The Paddy Roller's flaming eyes stilled, and the sky grew calm.

"Deal."

Chapter 29
The Last Shot

The wood and concrete beneath Theo's feet cracked, and he was tossed in the air. He fell for moments on end, until his feet landed on blacktop and he toppled forward. It was the basketball court next to the playground.

"Hmm. Interesting," the Paddy Roller mumbled. He snapped his fingers, and his hellhounds began to howl and stood up on their haunches. The sound of bones cracking split the air as their bodies contorted into half hound and half man. Werewolves.

"Some basketball shorts at least," Theo complained. The man snapped again, clothing the werewolves in matching jerseys.

"It's five on five," the Paddy Roller said, smiling.

"But it's just me here."

"You set the game. I set the terms. It's only fair. I guess you'll have to forfeit," he said smoothly, as if the matter was already settled and he'd already won.

They both turned as the gate to the court squealed and in walked—

"Great-Aunt Trudy Anne?!" Theo choked out.

"You ain't alone," she shouted. Instead of her shawl and housedress she sported a pair of balloon-like blue shorts, long socks, and a cotton jersey shirt with writing on the front.

Theo smiled. "You play basketball?"

"All-star point guard for the Bennett College Belles of 1959. Femi put out a call for help, and I can't leave my people alone. My ghost network let us know where to go."

"My cousin?" Theo asked, genuinely surprised.

"Family sticks together."

One of the werewolves barked, and the Paddy Roller leaned on his shotgun. "She don't have a body. Ain't gonna be much use."

"He got us."

It was Romare, Tariq, Vernon and, pulling up the rear, Femi.

"You didn't think we'd let you battle a demigod alone. You fam now! Baby couldn't make it, but sends his best," Tariq said. They all dapped him up until he came to Femi, who had his arms crossed against his chest.

"I apologize if I ever made you feel like you were any less than family. I realized that when you left. That—I been talking to New Nana and meditating with Aunt Ionie. I'm messed up. It's my fault, and I'm sorry."

"It's okay."

"No, it's not, but it will be."

Femi held out his fist for Theo but pulled him into a quick hug instead.

"Now let's clean this up. I got a date with Darryl later."

Theo turned around, a curious feeling of lightness in his chest. Love, that's what it was, filling him, restoring him, boosting him up. The Paddy Roller added two more ghouls, a restless ghost sheriff still in his uniform, his eyelids stitched shut with thin rusted wire. The other was a young woman, eerie in how normal she seemed among the rest of the grotesque crew, in a T-shirt and yoga pants.

The Paddy Roller snapped his fingers, and a silent audience filled the stands, old and young, the freshly dead still waiting to cross over, probably confused about where they were and what they were witnessing. Theo licked his lips and walked over to his team.

"All right, uh, I guess I'm the captain, so, Tariq, you're center, 'cause you're the tallest. Femi, you're the power forward. I'll be the small forward. Vernon, who's the best shooter, you or Romare?"

Vernon scoffed. "Me, of course."

Tariq's face shifted, and he tucked his hands under his armpits. "C'mon, man, be honest."

"Aight, Romare."

"Cool. Romare, you're the shooting guard, and Vernon, you're the point guard. I guess we gotta come up with some rules for the game. I mean, he's a demon and all. He ain't gonna play fair."

"The man got werewolves on this team. You know he ain't gonna play fair," Vernon said.

Femi chimed in. "Tell him no biting, scratching, or magic that blinds, bleeds, or levitates. Streetball rules, outside of that. Anything goes. We play to ten."

"Yo, Femi, you sound real ruthless right now," Tariq commented.

Femi shrugged. "Gotta be. We got too much riding on this."

"Um, how much is riding on this?" Romare asked.

Theo drew in a big breath. "Everything."

"What about a referee?" Romare asked. Theo was stumped. They definitely needed someone impartial.

"They can't be on one side or the other," Vernon chimed.

Tariq snapped his fingers. "I got it."

Theo's team lined up at the center for a faceoff.

"Homeboy ain't even trading in his boots for sneakers," Vernon quipped. Romare snickered.

"Nah, them Air Confederate 64s," Tariq retorted. Theo couldn't help snickering.

Theo drew himself up as tall as he could and raised his voice. "We got your five on five, but we got terms."

"Within reason, boy," the Paddy Roller replied. "Gonna be a short game. I'd like my ancestral home back right quick."

"It's gotta be a clean game. No biting, scratching, or magic, and we need an impartial referee."

"And?"

"We choose—" Tariq started, but Theo raised his hand. He knew this was a negotiation, and he couldn't start out with his main guy first, so he started with someone he knew would get rejected. A great basketball player, but also a great cantor and hypnotist.

"Prince."

The guys all looked at him like he was crazy. "Huh? You mean like *Purple Rain* Prince?"

Femi laughed, catching on to Theo's strategy.

"Robert Mugabe," the Roller replied.

"I can't verify his basketball cred," Theo answered. Who knew what bloody dictators did in their free time? Great-Aunt Trudy Anne came over and whispered in his ear. He countered again: "Kobe Bryant."

"Elegba."

Theo thought about that. Elegba was a trickster god and famously neutral to the whims of man, but he didn't know enough about him to say yes or no. He wasn't raised in the Yoruba and Candomble traditions. He nodded to Vernon, who practically shouted the next option.

"Death."

The flaming coals the demon used for eyes rolled in his skull as he thought. "So be it."

He snapped his fingers, and in a flash of flame, Death appeared. He was a skeleton with sickle in hand, sleek and sharp. He wore a shiny eggplant-colored striped three-piece suit, Stacy Adams alligator shoes, and a feathered hat.

"You best make this worth my while, little one," he said to Theo, his voice slick as oil. "Hmm, Old Tatterly versus New Tatterly."

Not five minutes later, everyone was ready to start. Theo had taken off his sweatshirt and piled it in the corner with Rupert. He'd be playing in a T-shirt, not that it mattered when he was standing opposite a blind sheriff, who he suspected could see just fine.

Death stood at center court, ball in hand, the Paddy Roller on one side and Tariq on the other.

Without a word, Death tossed the ball, and without much effort at all, the Paddy Roller snatched the rock out of the air. He passed to the blond girl, who brought it up court. The werewolves, one playing small forward and the other power, came in hard from opposite sides of the court toward the basket. With grace and an odd lightness, she brought the ball to the three-point line and tossed it in an alley-oop. One of the werewolves went for it, snatching it out of the air, and dunked, letting one paw hang on the rim, his tongue lolling out at the side.

Theo stood out of bounds with the ball after side-stepping one of the werewolves, who couldn't help snapping his jaws as he ran past. A quick dribble and he tossed it to Femi, who was unguarded and in a good position to hit a three if he was bold, but he never got the chance. Out of nowhere, the blind sheriff stole the ball mid-dribble and raced down the court, dipping and sliding like Kyrie Irving in cowboy boots. Romare somehow blocked the shot. The bad guys were still up by two.

"Don't get nervous," Femi said as he ran down the court.

Theo nodded. It was early. They had a chance. They did. He looked to the crowd. They didn't cheer; they didn't boo. They just sat and witnessed. Once again, Theo tossed the ball inside, this time to Tariq. The Paddy Roller was on him like skin on bone. Theo and Romare had an advantage, though: they were shorter than everyone else, and while the werewolves had wingspan, Theo had speed.

Claws reached out toward Theo's face, but he ducked and slid. He was open and made sure Tariq knew it, but the Paddy Roller was having none of it. Tariq couldn't pass to Theo, so he had to try the next best thing, which was Romare, who seemed to have a better shot, given that the sheriff guarding him was blind. Tariq faked left and then passed behind his back, sending the ball right to Romare, but the sheriff saw it coming and caught the ball with one hand. Romare stood shocked for a second too long as the sheriff jumped and shot for the three. They were down by five.

"We still got a chance. Keep ya head up," Vernon yelled as he guarded the girl. He had to spit to keep her ponytail out of his face. She was good. So good, Theo made a mental note to start watching more ladies' college ball, 'cause while the werewolves dunked, she shot, and before they knew it they were down by eight, just one shot away from losing it all. Theo raised his hand for a timeout.

The team gathered in a circle, Great-Aunt Trudy Anne at the center.

"You're down, but you ain't out. If you want to wiiiiiiin, you got to shout," she said.

"What's that supposed to mean?" Tariq asked.

"Do you believe you can win?" she asked them.

"Yeah?" Romare replied.

"I asked you," she said louder. "Do you believe you can win?"

All together they shouted. "Yeah!"

"Good, 'cause they whippin' y'all's tails out there, but I'm gone hip you to some Kareem Abdul-Jabbar game, some old Wilt Chamberlain seventy-six game, and a little Trudy Anne Tatterly circa 1957 game, 'cause I got strategy. Theo, I've been watching you practice those threes. You think you up to it?"

Theo nodded.

This time Femi tossed the ball in, with Romare shouting for all that he was worth that he was open.

"You think buckra can guard me? Old bleedy-face head folk. Nah," he yelled.

"Gotta grow some eyeballs if he really wanna guard you," Romare chimed in.

"I mean, I know y'all evil, but why you gotta be so ugly?" Vernon added. The werewolves growled, taking offense. It was just the opening Femi needed to shoot the ball to Theo, who quickly shot and made a three from almost half court. Great-Aunt Trudy Anne jumped nearly six feet in the air.

"Favor ain't fair!" she shouted.

The blind sheriff quickly rebounded and tossed the ball to one of the werewolves, but Femi was ready, ramming his body into the beast with all he had and slapping

259

the ball out of his grip. It bounced and was snatched by Tariq, who passed to Theo again.

He didn't even think. He shot. Another three.

With a growl, one of the werewolves rebounded and tossed to his brother. He barreled down the court, Femi hot on his heels. Death blew his whistle. Both teams looked toward him.

Death, as cool as he could be on a folding chair, crossed his legs. "Carrying."

The werewolf dropped to all fours and rushed him, but Death, who had been picking his teeth with a four-inch diamond-tipped needle, flicked it, sending the spike right into the werewolf's eye.

"Paddy, I suggest you get your dogs to heel. You asked for a fair game."

The Paddy Roller nodded. The werewolf picked the needle out of his eye and whimpered.

Femi had the ball and tossed it to Vernon, but the blond girl was quick and turned it over. She shot. Two points. Just two more points, and Theo's life and legacy was over.

It was a miss.

He exhaled as Femi got the ball and quickly shot for a three. Nine! They were at nine.

They just needed one more to win, but the Paddy Roller's eyes began to flame so hot they turned blue. He wasn't going to just roll over.

It was fast. Everything was moving too fast, and Theo needed to slow it down. He drew in a breath and blew it out slowly.

If you need to focus, you just need to breathe.

Aunt Ionie's voice came back to him, and suddenly, he really did begin to believe. He was playing a game against the most evil demigod in his region, with Death as the referee. He was special, and he knew it.

Boom. He tasted blood. One of the hounds had swiped him with an elbow, but Death hadn't seen. Theo spit blood and got his head together. Romare, who was being pounded by the sheriff, tossed him the ball, and with agility he didn't know he had, he slid under the stinking hellhound's legs and went for it.

"For Billy," Theo said as he took the shot. It arced through the air, bouncing once on the rim and then the backboard before falling through the net with a swish.

"Point. New Tatterly."

Chapter 30
The Aftermath

No applause, no roaring crowd, just disintegration. First the audience, then the court and the hellhounds, and finally, *finally* the Paddy Roller himself.

"Is he gone for real?" Theo asked as he picked himself up from the aquarium floor. No one answered. He was alone. The votive candles he'd lit had burned out, and it was dark. He checked his pocket, and Rupert was there, small and unassuming. Miss Purrkins busied herself rubbing against his legs.

"Did I just dream all that?" he said out loud, but then he shook his head. His body hurt. He was covered in sweat, and he'd never been hungrier in all his life. It was dark. He could hear the jackhammer of renewed construction outside, so he followed the sounds to the closest exit door and pushed it open. The light nearly blinded him, right before Issa picked him up off his feet with a bone-crushing hug.

"You're a maniac!" she yelled as his team clapped and rushed up.

"'Bout time you made it out. We've been out here nearly twenty minutes. Thought maybe you didn't make it like we saw," Romare said, a smile splitting his face. He was holding his mother's hand tight, like he was afraid she was gonna blow away. "I've never used my astral self before. It was cool."

"I'm sorry I sprayed you," Theo said to Ms. Carlisle, and she waved her hand at him.

"I was not myself. I don't think I've been myself for a while. I don't even like black."

A car horn honked loudly, and they all turned to see all the aunties pile out of the van, Issa's mom first.

"Issa!" Aunt Thalia shouted. Theo let Issa go to run over to her mom, Miss Purrkins nestled in her arms.

Theo knew he'd be on punishment until he hit graduation.

"I guess that's the end of my very short basketball career," he mumbled. Femi lightly punched him in the arm.

"Nah, I'll bet the aunties go light on you this time. I mean, you did save the family line, rescue Issa from certain death, and play the best game of your life."

"But we didn't get the deed."

"We'll find it. Relax. You should be proud of yourself. I am."

"Bruh, you're embarrassing me. I don't know how to feel with you being all nice to me and stuff."

"Oh, that's just for today, Sno—I mean, Theo."

Theo tried to think of something else to say, but kept coming up blank. It didn't matter, though, because a cop car was pulling up right behind the aunties.

"Time to go," Vernon yelled. Romare started howling.

"That's what our team name shoulda been. The Howlers."

It was game night. Femi was right. The aunties did go light on him, but that didn't mean there were no consequences. They were just feeling lighter after it was revealed that Dr. Rollins was only on vacation, and Romare's mom returned the original deed to Tatterly Place to Aunt Sabrina. She couldn't remember how she'd gotten it and blamed it on a research mixup with the #nogentinchucktown campaign.

Theo's mom put up an ironclad ward on the windows and doors so that nothing got in or out, including him. It was two weeks of a mini quarantine and a serious discussion about him attending the famous Boys' Academy of Magic in Tuskegee. She hadn't made a decision on it yet, but even he had to admit that a little formal magical instruction wouldn't hurt. But for the time being, all was normal, and he didn't have to quit the basketball team.

It was raining, one of those first really cold rains of the season, and the smell of crab bisque and garlic bread was wafting throughout the house. Femi and Issa were playing Breath of the Wild, and Uncle Tope and Uncle Mack were deep into a game of dominoes. As for Theo, he was placing a card with his face on it at the top of the precarious card castle he'd built with the new deck Uncle Mack had gifted to Aunt Cedella.

"Uncle Mack. Where'd you get these cards?" he asked.

Without looking up from his black and white oracles, he replied, "My sister runs a printing side business. Last time I wanted to play some spades up in here, y'all didn't have nothing to play it with."

Aunt Sabrina laughed as she poured out a bowl of the bisque for New Nana to try. She'd only spent one night in the hospital. Rupert was resting in her lap.

"Card games are common," New Nana replied. "You should let Cedella teach you how to play chess."

Aunt Cedella poked her tongue out at Theo as she took Aunt Ionie's bishop.

"Though it is a nice set of cards," Ro offered. "The artwork is lovely, though I object to my face being used as the joker."

"I don't," Aunt Cedella said just as Theo's finger slipped, bringing the house of cards down completely.

Aunt Sabrina jumped up, drew in a shocked breath, and dropped the glass of water she'd just poured for New Nana. It shattered on the floor, causing everyone to turn and look. She pointed in Theo's direction, panic and realization on her face.

"What's wrong, Bri?" Theo's mom asked. Aunt Ionie ran to get the broom and mop.

"Y'all don't move. I don't want anyone cutting themselves."

A tear rolled down Aunt Sabrina's face as she clutched her chest and laughed.

"This was my vision," she said.

"What vision?" Uncle Mack asked.

"The vision of Theo bringing down the House of Tatterly. It was the cards. The cards are the House of Tatterly."

Everyone, even Theo, drew in a breath of relief. The premonition had been hanging over them, and Theo was sure he'd thwarted the message, but here it was. She was right.

"I told you all. My Sabrina is always right," New Nana added, then she kissed Rupert's scaly head.

Acknowledgments

There are so many people to thank, but I want to thank my husband Jovan, my nephews Tate and Bryce, my daddy, and all my uncles and cousins who live in an America that doesn't recognize how magical they are, but who show me how to be brave and soft every day. I want to thank my agent, John, who never turns away any of my ideas and all the people who make books possible. There are so many people behind the scenes who illustrate the cover and call booksellers to pitch my book. Suzy, Marcie, Ronique, Darby, Jenny, Chris, and Daniel, you're amazing. There are the line editors and the people who format. There are so many hands that a manuscript has to go through before it hits the shelf, and I am so grateful to them and to God that I get to share stories and spread joy into this world, and I pray I get to continue to do it for years to come.

About the Author

Shanna Miles was born and raised in Columbia, South Carolina, and considers herself a dyed-in-the-wool Southern girl. She lives in Georgia with her family. When she's not working as a high school librarian, she can be found writing about magical Black boys. Visit her online at shannamiles.net or on Twitter at @srmilesauthor.